D1348684

2301205

F/2301205

PORTRAIT OF A MAN
(*LE CONDOTTIÈRE*)

GEORGES PEREC

PORTRAIT OF A MAN
(*LE CONDOTTIÈRE*)

*Translated from the French
and with an introduction by
David Bellos*

MACLEHOSE PRESS
QUERCUS · LONDON

First published in the French language as *Le Condottière*
by Éditions de Seuil, Paris, 2012
First published in Great Britain in 2014 by

MacLehose Press
an imprint of Quercus
55 Baker Street
7th Floor, South Block
London W1U 8EW

Ouvrage publié avec le concours du Ministère français chargé de la Culture –
Centre national du livre

ISBN (HB) 978 0 85705 238 4
ISBN (Ebook) 978 1 78206 095 6

10 9 8 7 6 5 4 3 2 1

Designed and typeset in Cycles by Libanus Press, Marlborough
Printed and bound in Great Britain by Clays Ltd, St Ives plc

INTRODUCTION

From a passage in his disturbing autobiographical fiction, *W or The Memory of Childhood*, first published in 1975, readers have long known that Georges Perec's "first more or less completed novel" dealt with a famous painting by the fifteenth-century Italian artist Antonello da Messina, the *Portrait of a Man known as* Il Condottiere (1475). However, no such novel was published in Perec's lifetime. When I started to gather material for a biography of the writer a few years after he died in 1982, there was no trace of it in his surviving papers. Like other early titles listed in the "autobibliography" that Perec compiled in 1989 for the literary magazine *L'Arc*, the "Antonello novel" was missing.

Old friends of the writer and the letters they'd kept and allowed me to read soon told me what had happened to these unfindable works. Georges Perec, born 1936, published his breakthrough novel, *Things*, in 1965. Partly through word of mouth and partly through the award of the Renaudot Prize, it flew off the shelves, and was hailed as the mirror of the rising generation. Perec, who had a poorly paid day job as librarian in a medical research laboratory, suddenly found himself a literary celebrity, and in a position to leave his thirty-five-square-metre perch in Rue de Quatrefages (reimagined and just slightly displaced in *Things*) for a larger home in Rue du Bac. Preparing for the move in spring 1966, he stuffed redundant paperwork into a cardboard suitcase intended for the dump, and put his literary papers in a different case of similar appearance. In the move, the wrong case got junked. All of Perec's manuscripts and typescripts prior to the writing of *Things* disappeared.

The story led me to expect I would never get to read those lost works. What I set out to do as Perec's first biographer was to talk to as many people as I could who had known the writer during his tragically short life. My pursuit of biographical information led me to Belgrade, just before the collapse of Yugoslavia, to meet several Serbian artists and scholars who had befriended Perec during their time as graduate students in Paris in the 1950s. Two of them had hung on to carbon copies of some of those lost works, including a short story, *Manderre*, and a novel entitled *L'Attentat de Sarajevo*, that remain unpublished. However, the Yugoslavs had all left Paris in 1956 or 1957 on the expiry of their scholarships. They hadn't heard of anything like an "Antonello novel".

The following year, when I'd already drafted the first part of *Georges Perec. A Life in Words*, there were only a few names left on my list of people to see, and I didn't expect that they would add much to the wealth of information that Perec's many other friends had already shared with me. Following up the remaining leads that I had, I went to dine with a former journalist who'd met Perec at the Moulin d'Andé, the writer's retreat in Normandy that was Perec's second home in the later 1960s. Towards the end of the evening, as I was looking for an opportunity to make my escape, Alain Guérin let it out that someone had once given him one of Perec's pieces to look at. He didn't know if it was of any interest. Could I perhaps tell him what it was? Guérin went to a wardrobe, pulled out a manila envelope and handed it to me. There it was: 157 carbon copy sheets of flimsy paper beginning: *georges perec le condottiere roman* (ee cummings-style lower-case was fashionable among the French avant-garde in those days). I told Guérin it was immensely precious – but could I please take it away to read? With great generosity he allowed me to do just that, and I stayed up all night reading Perec's "first more or less completed novel" in bed. It was really hard to follow – I put it down to the late hour, the smudgy carbon and the dim hotel lighting. But before my bleary eyes finally shut, I knew that I had in my hands the unhoped-for revelation of the tangled roots of Perec's later creation and of the masterwork that crowns it. However, I have to admit that even after a good night's sleep, in good light and clear print, *Portrait of a Man* remains hard to follow. It is connected by a hundred threads to every part of the literary universe that Perec went on to create – but it's not like anything else that he wrote.

The story isn't particularly elaborate. Gaspard Winckler, born around 1930, is dispatched by his well-to-do French parents to a boarding school in Switzerland during the war. A young and wealthy idler with a good eye and outstanding manual skills, he falls in with a painter called Jérôme, who trains him to become a high-class forger of artworks of every kind. Winckler breaks off relations with his family, acquires qualifications in art restoration and a dummy job in a museum to cover his tracks, and then spends twelve years in well-remunerated employment faking coins, jewellery and oil paintings ranging from Renaissance Madonnas to Impressionist landscapes. Anatole Madera, the head of the international gang of dealers that trades Winckler's output, then asks him to use a wooden panel painted by a minor Renaissance figure to forge a new master-piece by someone sufficiently famous to command a very high price. Winckler selects Antonello da Messina as his target, for financial, art-historical and personal reasons. However, he conceives of the commission as the ultimate challenge. He aims not to pastiche an existing portrait, but to make an entirely new one that would be accepted as an Antonello by buyers and experts and would also be a work of art in its own right. A work devoid of artistic merit could hardly be seen as an Antonello, of course; but Winckler's ambition is to create something that is simultaneously Antonello's and his own authentic creation. Predictably, the result falls short of such a high mark. Rebelling against a failure he'd set up himself, Winckler cuts Madera's throat. Perec's account begins at this point when, having murdered his paymaster, Winckler finds himself trapped in a base-ment studio. He tunnels his way out, and returns to Yugoslavia to tell his story once again to Streten, an old (and apparently older) friend. That's it. We never learn what happened next.

The story is told twice: first, as an internal monologue, in a bewildering variety of stream-of-consciousness techniques, while Winckler digs himself out of Madera's house at Dampierre, in the countryside near Dreux (Eure-et-Loir), about an hour from Paris; then in speech, in a Q. & A. session halfway between police interrogation and psychotherapy. Perec often returned to the formal idea of the two-part work: *W or The Memory of Childhood* has alternating chapters that tell apparently different stories, and his unfinished detective novel, *"53 Days"*, was designed to have a second part that would undo everything set up in the first. In both narrations of the first Gaspard Winckler's plight, murder is presented as the key to liberation. It's the means by which Winckler can cease to be a fake artist in both senses of the phrase – as a maker of fakes, and as a false artist. Mortal violence is what he needs to begin to be himself.

Gaspard Winckler is also the name of the craftsman in *Life A User's Manual* who cuts Percival Bartlebooth's five hundred water-colours into increasingly difficult jigsaw puzzles. Chapter One of that great novel is located on the stairs of 11 Rue Simon-Crubellier. An estate agent is on her way to inspect Winckler's now vacant apartment. "Gaspard Winckler is dead, but the long and meticulous, patiently laid plot of his revenge is not finished yet." Though we may never quite be sure what the real end or purpose of that plot is, we now know what set it in train: the anger provoked by an artist's failure to create an authentic *Portrait of a Man*.

Perec would have liked to be a painter, but he was all fingers and thumbs. He had an outstandingly good eye all the same, and his works often revolve around painting in one form or another. *Things* begins with a meticulous description of a stylishly decorated dream-home; *A Gallery Portrait*, Perec's last completed work, deals with a painting that represents a collection of paintings, all of which turn out to be fakes. Perec's painterly imagination reaches its apex in *Life A User's Manual* which is, simultaneously and undecidably, a portrait of all the rooms in a Parisian apartment house that a painter called Serge Valène would like to put on canvas, and a description of the painting that Valène has barely begun to sketch out.

Perec's education in visual art began among the Yugoslav group he attached himself to in Paris around 1955, of which the most striking trace is a portrait of Perec by the Serbian artist Mladen Srbinović. It continued apace among the young intellectuals who formed Perec's second circle in the later 1950s and with whom he sought to launch a new cultural periodical under the title *The General Line* (which never appeared). Alone and with friends, Perec visited exhibitions and galleries in Paris and made a trip to Berne to see a large collection of works by Paul Klee. But the Antonello portrait that hangs in the seven-metre gallery in the Louvre was a special favourite, for a quite peculiar reason. Like his hero Gaspard, Perec had been at a boarding school in the Alps during the war, where he was taught to ski. Around the age of eight or nine, he had an accident in the changing room:

> One of my skis slipped from my hand and accidentally grazed the face of the boy putting his skis away next to me and he, in a mad fury, picked up one of his ski sticks and hit me with it on the face ... cutting open my upper lip ... The scar that resulted from this attack is still perfectly visible today ... It became a personal mark ... It is this scar also

which gave me a particular preference . . . for Antonello da
Messina's *Portrait of a Man known as* Il Condottiere. (p. 108)

The scar on the ancient canvas is not much like the graze on Perec's
upper lip (one is dead centre above the lip, the other to the left and
bisects the lip itself). I suspect that the reason given by Perec covers
another and perhaps more important one. Most postcard reproductions of the Antonello portrait show only the face of the unknown
sitter (whether he really was a *condottiere*, a leader or warlord, or just
an accountant or a chum is a matter of conjecture). However,
Antonello also painted a false frame at the base (but not on the three
other sides), and on it he depicted a strip of folded paper bearing
the Latin inscription *Antonellus Messaneus me pinxit*: "Antonella of
Messina painted me". The *cartellino* or caption panel also says
without saying that Antonello also painted "Antonello painted me":
a self-confirming loop that indirectly but no less clearly asserts the
artist's ownership of his work.

Perec was a modest and unassuming man in real life, but in
his art he was at least as self-assertive as his Renaissance model.

He would be in the painting himself in the manner of
those Renaissance painters who reserved for themselves a
tiny place in the crowd of vassals, soldiers, bishops and
burghers; not a central place . . . but an apparently inoffen-
sive place . . . as if it were only supposed to be a signature
to be read by initiates, something like a mark which the

> commissioning buyer would only just tolerate the painter
> signing his work with . . . (*Life A User's Manual*, p. 226)

Gaspard's dilemma is this. An authentic work of art expresses its creator's grasp of the world and of himself, by definition; whereas a successful fake of an artwork seems to express the world-view of someone other than its creator, namely, of the artist whose work is being imitated. Therefore, however perfect it is from a technical point of view, a painting cannot be a forgery and an authentic work of art at the same time. Winckler, who doesn't have Perec's taste for logical exegesis (or the benefit of dialectical debate with Marxist friends) learns this only slowly, from experience. He sets out to achieve the impossible feat of creating a real masterpiece that will be recognised (and therefore purchased) as a genuine Antonello. But by the very fact of his success in "painting like Antonello", Winckler, like Antonello before him, produces an authentic image of his own true self – an evasive, indeterminate fraud of no fixed identity. The more "like" the process is, the less "like" the product can be. He's cooked. He's done for. He's finished. Perec doesn't explain the argument of his novel half so clearly because he wants to take his readers through the process by which a false artist comes face to face with the truth of art. This is a novel, not an essay. Almost.

Superficially, *Portrait of a Man* isn't like any of Perec's later works, but just as significantly it isn't much like any other French fiction of the 1950s either. It seems as unrelated in its manner to the "new novels" of Alain Robbe-Grillet (*The Erasers*, 1953; *Jealousy*,

1957) as it is to the politically committed fiction that Sartre and Beauvoir had launched in the 1940s (*The Roads to Freedom*, 1945–1949; *The Mandarins*, 1954). Because its first part consists of internal monologue in a basement room, it may owe something to Dostoevsky's *Notes from the Underground*, but the comparison doesn't lead very far. The fact that it adopts (and adapts) stream-of-consciousness technique doesn't mean Perec was thinking of Virginia Woolf (or that he had read her work, which I doubt). The nearest though still distant analogue to it is Michel Butor's *Modification* (1957), which uses the second-person form of address to recreate the process by which a man becomes aware of where his future path lies. All Perec's later work is in constant and intense dialogue with literary tradition; but *Portrait of a Man* engages with the matter of writing indirectly, through the tangled concepts of authenticity and the real as they can be articulated in pictorial art.

After adding a chapter about the first Gaspard Winckler to my biography of Perec, I returned the precious typescript to Alain Guérin, who later placed it in a public collection. A second carbon copy was then found among the papers of another one of Perec's friends of the 1950s. With the discovery of other texts believed lost in the move from Rue de Quatrefages and the publication of substantial parts of Perec's correspondence from the 1950s, a fuller, richer picture of "Perec before Perec" began to emerge. But there was understandable reluctance to publish his juvenilia. That's what happens to writers thoroughly dead and gone. Perec may have passed away in 1982, but his work and his personality remained a living part of contemporary literature for many decades after that. And still today.

In this respect *Portrait of a Man* is an exceptional text. It's true it was rejected and then lost, but it certainly doesn't belong to the category of "teenage experiment" or "youthful folly". It wasn't dashed off in a burst like *L'Attentat de Sarajevo*, nor was it left incomplete. It's the result of a process of drafting and revision that lasted around three years, before, during and after Perec's military service in a parachute regiment. In 1958 a version called *Gaspard pas mort* ("Gaspard Not Dead") was submitted to a publishing house that turned it down, but an editor at France's most prestigious literary publisher, Gallimard, got to hear of it. He was sufficiently impressed to issue a contract in 1959 – with an advance on royalties, to boot! But he thought it not quite ready for publication, and asked Perec to revise it. On his release from the military in December 1959, Perec set to work, and when he'd finished rewriting it one more time eight months later, he was so thoroughly exhausted with his *condottière* that he wrote ENDENDENDEND across a whole line on the last page, followed by a warning in uppercase:

YOU'LL HAVE TO PAY ME LOADS IF YOU WANT
ME TO START IT OVER AGAIN. Thursday, 25 August,
1960.

He was in a hurry to finish because he was about to leave for Sfax, in Tunisia, where his wife Paulette had got a job as a teacher under a cultural co-operation scheme between France and its former protectorate. The dreadful news came in a letter from Gallimard just a few days before they left Paris. Having read the new version, they preferred not to proceed with the contract. Perec did not need to return the advance.

The blow nearly knocked the young writer off his perch. The months that followed were among the gloomiest in all Perec's adult life. But he picked himself up, and began several new projects before alighting on the path that would lead him to *Things*. As he wrote to a friend in 1960, "Best of luck to anyone who reads [my novel]. I'll go back to it in ten years when it'll turn into a masterpiece, or else I'll wait in my grave until one of my faithful exegetes comes across it in an old trunk you once owned and brings it out." *Perec me pinxit*, I suppose.

What ties Perec's first novel to its period most visibly is the topic of forgery. In 1945, a Dutch art dealer called Han van Meegeren was arrested for having sold extremely important Dutch paintings, including several Vermeers, to Nazi occupiers during the war. His defence at trial was quite flabbergasting: he denied selling any national treasures, because the works he admitted selling to Nazi top brass were his own. He'd forged everything! Far from being a collaborator, he'd succeeded in hoodwinking the enemy. To prove he was a forger he even painted a new Vermeer in his cell, under the eyes of experts and guards.

The van Meegeren affair revived discussion of earlier art scams by Alceo Dossena, the "man with the magic hands", who'd come clean in 1928 because he reckoned he'd been duped by his own dealers, and by Joni Federico Icilio, who'd hoodwinked Bernard Berenson as well as many major museums before revealing himself in a book released in 1937. What exactly was the difference between an authentic work of art and its perfect imitation? Books and articles flowed from learned and opinionated pens on this issue in the 1950s. In 1955, an exhibition of fake art was held at the Grand Palais in Paris, where Perec no doubt saw some of the works by Icilio, Dossena, and van Meegeren that he mentions in *Portrait of a Man*. It was sponsored by the Paris Prefecture of Police – probably the only police force in the world that puts on art shows!

The police had their own reason for being interested in fakes, but arguments over the difference between *fake* and *authentic* had other resonances for Perec and his circle. "Authentic" is a central term in the existential philosophy of Jean-Paul Sartre, who was then at the height of his prestige. Sartre's epochal pamphlet of 1945, *Réflexions sur la question juive* (translated as *Anti-Semite and Jew*), makes a firm distinction between the "authentic Jew" and the "inauthentic" one. The "inauthentic Jew" was constructed as a Jew solely by the gaze of other people; inauthenticity consisted in accepting a given role as "the Other". "Authenticity", in Sartre's terminology, means the full assumption of an identity by an act of will and choice. Like many of his friends, Perec was of Jewish heritage, and in the Sartrean atmosphere of the Left Bank in the 1950s, the issue of authenticity was not just a philosophical matter. Perec's struggle with fakery in his first novel isn't just about the history of European art.

But it is also about art, and draws on extensive learning. Perec read Alexandre Ziloty's classic study of the origins of oil painting, and quotes verbatim in Italian from Vasari's *Lives of the Painters* (though mostly from the parts that Ziloty also quotes). He certainly had access to the catalogue of the 1955 exhibition, and he obtained other knowledge from the Yugoslav art historians he had befriended in Paris, one of whom studied the Roman treasures unearthed in 1953 at Gamzigrad (Felix Romuliana, now a World Heritage Site). These more or less well absorbed snippets of art history enabled him to integrate an imaginary character, Gaspard Winckler, into what was then known of the contemporary art forgery business, and to patchwork a plausible scam out of elements copied from real ones, in a process of composition uncannily similar to the way van Meegeren had patchworked features of existing masterpieces to produce new ones for sale. Perec would later transpose this technique from thematic material to literary composition, reproducing (and sometimes modifying) actual fragments of sentences already written by Flaubert in *Things*, and then, more ambitiously, snippets of Melville, Kafka, Duras, Le Clézio and many others in *A Man Asleep*, and finally, in *Life A User's Manual*, constructing a vast programmatic insertion of hidden quotations from a score of authors in prose that remained indisputably his own.

I have translated the text of the novel as it was published in French in 2012, thirty years after Perec's death. In some places where the typescript has a different and more acceptable reading, I have relied on Perec's original words. I've also restored the division into parts, which the French editors decided to suppress. For the title, I have adopted the name by which Antonello's panel is known to art historians in English rather than reproduce Perec's original *Condottière*, with its anomalous grave accent, since it is not a French work. That choice also points the reader to the book's effective subject. What Winckler discovers is that a portrait of a man is always a portrait of the artist; what Perec told his editor Maurice Nadeau at a crucial juncture in his writing career ten years after abandoning this novel was that autobiography "is the only kind of writing possible".

The greatest difficulty this text sets for translation into English is the distinction that we make between "conscience" – the moral faculty of discriminating between right and wrong – and "consciousness", the faculty or state of being aware. These two different things are represented by only one word of French, *la conscience*. This regular mismatch between the two languages produces numerous forks in a novel whose narrator often asks himself: "What use is a *conscience*?" The problem can hardly be evaded, especially as in Perec's own stated view *Portrait of a Man* is *l'histoire d'une conscience*. In many cases it's clear which of the two meanings is dominant, and the appropriate translation relates to "being aware" (of oneself, of the world). However, there are a sufficient number of undecidable cases to make any English-language translation of Perec's first novel an interpretation as well as a reproduction of Gaspard Winckler's silent and spoken struggle.

The text also contains some extremely long sentences. I've done my best to respect the complex syntax of these bravura passages, but despite its renowned flexibility, English can't quite manage all the soaring flights of Perec's intellectual rhetoric. In some cases all that's needed is a slight change in the order of the clauses; but in others, I felt I had to take the sentence apart and put it back together in a different shape. Later on, Perec got a better grip on the art of the multiply nested sentence: his investigation of all the things you can do with an X in *W or The Memory of Childhood* (p. 72), like the 17-line description of the background of the 439th puzzle that Bartlebooth has just failed to complete in the last chapter of *Life A User's Manual* (p. 494) – require careful attention for translation into English, but don't need to be recast. The convoluted multi-clause sentences of *Portrait of a Man* are more like exercises preparing Perec for greater exploits to come.

What's disconcerting is the rejection of a single narrative voice. Winckler "talks" in Part I in the first, second and third persons, alternating between them according to no perceptible plan or logic. This intentional instability may be what Gallimard's rejection letter meant to refer to when it cited "excessive clumsiness and chatter" in the text, but there's no doubt that some members of its distinguished panel of readers really didn't like Perec's taste for puns in a serious novel about an art forger's crisis of conscience.

In *Les Misérables*, Victor Hugo described puns as *la fiente de l'esprit*, "the guano of the mind". Most people think he meant to deride word games as intellectual waste, but a few who respect the esteem in which the great author held human excrement (Valjean's famous escape through the sewers is preceded by a serious proposal

to recycle the shit of Paris as fertiliser) believe that he really meant to say that puns *enrich* the mind's loam. Perec was of the second persuasion, without any doubt. In daily life and in his literary work, Perec was an incessant player of word games, and he coined some of the most memorable puns in the French language. In *Portrait of A Man*, he drops in a few that oblige the translator to compete. What they're doing here is in one respect quite obvious. Bewildering though they may have been to his first readers, Perec's verbal quips have become the most recognisable part of his first finished portrait of himself.

David Bellos

Princeton, December 2013

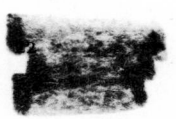

PORTRAIT OF A MAN
(*LE CONDOTTIÈRE*)

For Jacques Lederer

Like many men, I have made my descent into Hell, and, like some, I have more or less returned from it.

MICHEL LEIRIS, *Manhood*

And, in the first place, I will recall to my mind the things I have hitherto held as true, because perceived by the senses, and the foundations upon which my belief in their truth rested; I will, in the second place, examine the reasons that afterward constrained me to doubt of them; and, finally, I will consider what of them I ought now to believe.

DESCARTES, *Meditations*

I

Madera was heavy. I grabbed him by the armpits and went backwards down the stairs to the laboratory. His feet bounced from tread to tread in a staccato rhythm that matched my own unsteady descent, thumping and banging around the narrow stairwell. Our shadows danced on the walls. Blood was still flowing, all sticky, seeping from the soaking wet towel, rapidly forming drips on the silk lapels, then disappearing into the folds of the jacket, like trails of slightly glinting snot side-tracked by the slightest roughness in the fabric, sometimes accumulating into drops that fell to the floor and exploded into star-shaped stains. I let him slump at the bottom of the stairs, right next to the laboratory door, and then went back up to fetch the razor and to mop up the bloodstains before Otto returned. But Otto came in by the other door at almost the same time as I did. He looked at me uncomprehendingly. I beat a retreat, ran down the stairs, and shut myself in the laboratory. I padlocked the door and jammed the wardrobe up against it. He came down a few minutes later, tried to force the door open, to no avail, then went back upstairs, dragging Madera behind him. I reinforced the door with the easel. He called out to me. He fired at the door twice with his revolver.

You see, maybe you told yourself it would be easy. Nobody in the house, no-one round and about. If Otto hadn't come back so soon, where would you be? You don't know, you're here. In the same laboratory as ever, and nothing's changed, or almost nothing. Madera is dead. So what? You are still in the same underground studio, it's just a bit less tidy and bit less clean. The same light of day seeps through the basement window. The Condottiere, crucified on his easel . . .

He had looked all around. It was the same office – the same glass table-top, the same telephone, the same calendar on its chrome-plated steel base. It still had the stark orderliness and uncluttered iciness of an intentionally cold style, with strictly matching colours – dark green carpet, mauve leather armchairs, light brown wall covering – giving a sense of discreet impersonality with its large metal filing cabinets . . . But all of a sudden the flabby mass of Madera's body seemed grotesque, like a wrong note, something incoherent, anachronistic . . . He'd slipped off his chair and was lying on his back with his eyes half closed and his slightly parted lips stuck in an expression of idiotic stupor enhanced by the dull gleam of a gold tooth. Blood streamed from his cut throat in thick spurts and trickled onto the floor, gradually soaking into the carpet, making an ill-defined, blackish stain that grew ever larger around his head, around his face whose whiteness had long seemed rather fishy, a warm, living, animal stain slowly taking possession of the room, as if the walls were already soaked through with it, as if the orderliness and strictness had already been overturned, abolished, pillaged, as if nothing more existed beyond the radiating stain and the obscene and ridiculous heap on the floor, the corpse, fulfilled, multiplied, made infinite . . .

Why? Why had he said that sentence: "I don't think that'll be a problem"? He tries to recall the precise tone of Madera's voice, the timbre that had taken him by surprise the first time he'd heard it, that slight lisp, its faintly hesitant intonation, the almost imperceptible limp in his words, as if he were stumbling – almost tripping – as if he were permanently afraid of making a mistake. I don't think. What nationality? Spanish? South American? Accent? Put on? Tricky. No. Simpler than that: he rolled his *r*s in the back of his throat. Or perhaps he was just a bit hoarse? He can see him coming towards him with outstretched hand: "Gaspard – that's what I should call you, isn't it? – I'm truly delighted to make your acquaintance." So what? It didn't mean much to him. What was he doing here? What did the man want of him? Rufus hadn't warned him . . .

People always make mistakes. They think things will work out, will go on as per normal. But you never can tell. It's so easy to delude yourself. What do *you* want, then? An oil painting? You want a top-of-the-range Renaissance piece? Can do. Why not a *Portrait of a Young Man*, for instance . . .

A flabby, slightly over-handsome face. His tie. "Rufus has told me a lot about you." So what? Big deal! You should have paid attention, you should have been wary . . . A man you didn't know from Adam or Eve . . . But you rushed headlong to accept the opportunity. It was too easy. And now. Well, now . . .

This is where it had got him. He did the sums in his head: all that had been spent setting up the laboratory, including the cost of materials and reproductions – photographs, enlargements, X-ray images, images seen through Wood's lamp and with side-illumination – and the spotlights, the tour of European art galleries, upkeep ... a fantastic outlay for a farcical conclusion ... But what was comical about his idiotic incarceration? He was at his desk as if nothing had happened ... That was yesterday ... But upstairs there was Madera's corpse in a puddle of blood ... and Otto's heavy footsteps as he paced up and down keeping guard. All that to get to this! Where would he be now if ... He thinks of the sunny Balearic Islands – it would have taken just a wave of his hand a year and half before – Geneviève would be at his side ... the beach, the setting sun ... a picture postcard scene ... Is this where it all comes to a full stop?

Now he recalled every move he'd made. He'd just lit a cigarette, he was standing with one hand on the table, with his weight on one hip. He was looking at the *Portrait of a Man*. Then he'd stubbed out his cigarette quickly and his left hand had swept over the table, stopped, gripped a piece of cloth, and crumpled it tight – an old handkerchief used as a brush-rag. Everything was hazy. He was putting ever more of his weight onto the table without letting the Condottiere out of his sight. Days and days of useless effort? It was as if his weariness had given way to the anger rising in him, step by certain step. He was crushing the fabric in his hand and his nails had scored the wooden table-top. He had pulled himself up, gone to his work bench, rummaged among his tools ...

A black sheath made of hardened leather. An ebony handle. A shining blade. He had raised it to the light and checked the cutting edge. What had he been thinking of? He'd felt as if there was nothing in the world apart from that anger and that weariness ... He'd flopped into the armchair, put his head in his hands, with the razor scarcely a few inches from his eyes, set off clearly and sharply by the dangerously smooth surface of the Condottiere's doublet. A single movement and then curtains ... One thrust would be enough ... His arm raised, the glint of the blade ... a single movement ... he would approach slowly and the carpet would muffle the sound of his steps, he would steal up on Madera from behind ...

A quarter of an hour had gone by, maybe. Why did he have an impression of distant gestures? Had he forgotten? Where was he? He'd been upstairs. He'd come back down. Madera was dead. Otto was keeping guard. What now? Otto was going to phone Rufus, Rufus would come. And then? What if Otto couldn't get hold of Rufus? Where was Rufus? That's what it all hung on. On this stupid what-if. If Rufus came, he would die, and if Otto didn't get hold of Rufus, he would live. How much longer? Otto had a weapon. The skylight was too high and too small. Would Otto fall asleep? Does a man on guard need to sleep? ...

He was going to die. The thought of it comforted him like a promise. He was alive, he was going to be dead. Then what? Leonardo is dead, Antonello is dead, and I'm not feeling too well myself. A stupid death. A victim of circumstance. Struck down by bad luck, a wrong move, a mistake. Convicted in absentia. By unanimous decision with one abstention – which one? – he was sentenced to die like a rat in a cellar, under a dozen unfeeling eyes – the side lights and X-ray lamps purchased at outrageous prices from the laboratory at the Louvre – sentenced to death for murder by virtue of that good old moral legend of the eye, the tooth and the turn of the wheel – Achilles' wheel – death is the beginning of the life of the mind – sentenced to die because of a combination of circumstances, an incoherent conjunction of trivial events . . . Across the globe there were wires and submarine cables . . . Hello, Paris, this is Dreux, hold the line, we're connecting to Dampierre. Hello, Dampierre, Paris calling. You can talk now. Who could have imagined those peaceable operators with their earpieces becoming implacable executioners? . . . Hello, Monsieur Koenig, Otto speaking, Madera has just died . . .

In the dark of night the Porsche will leap forward with its head-lights spitting fire like dragons. There will be no accident. In the middle of the night they will come and get him . . .

And then? What the hell does it matter to you? They'll come and get you. Next? Slump into an armchair and stare long and hard until death overtakes into the eyes of the tall joker with the shiv, the ineffable Condottiere. Responsible or not responsible? Guilty or not guilty? I'm not guilty, you'll scream when they drag you up to the guillotine. We'll soon see about that, says the executioner. And down the blade comes with a clunk. Curtains. Self-evident justice. Isn't that obvious? Isn't it normal? Why should there be any other way out?

He'd been standing a bit like an idiot right in the middle of the salon when he saw her come into the hallway and then hesitate at the door, presumably because she had just noticed his presence, before turning firmly towards Rufus with Juliette in her wake (the latter seeming somewhat overwhelmed by events) – What did he do? He'd not stirred. He'd taken advantage of the fact that he was in relative shadow, as far from the flaming hearth as he was from the lamps at the bar, to keep quite still. Impassive. The one thing not to do. The last thing he should have done. Not the slightest movement. The reflex of dignity. What did dignity have to do with it? The best way to turn something that, an instant before, might still have seemed a mere misunderstanding into an insurmountable obstacle. Why had he suddenly turned to stone? Since he'd been expecting her for an hour or more while nonetheless pretending to get Rufus and Juliette to confirm that she wasn't coming, it was downright hypocritical of him to pretend to be surprised and stand stock still like a circus dog! Was he nailed or screwed to the floor? His strange posture in the middle of the room with a glass in his hand, dignified and attentive, draped in his dignity, striving to mislead by adopting the stiff and abstracted pose of a drunk, but not being very good at it he paid more attention to his own heartbeat, not daring to look anywhere, not daring even to finish his drink. He could have said something, or shouted, or screamed. He could have gone up to her. He might have done anything he chose. But he didn't. Not a twitch. He didn't even frown, blink, or breathe in.

His arm raised, the glint of the blade. He'd collapsed in a heap, drowning in his own blood. Stout, flabby, a healthy complexion. Then flopping down the stairs in his stained shirt and a bloody towel round his neck, like a slowly deflating red balloon . . .

You know nothing. You thought you were a champion. You thought it had happened. Your heady moment to have the world in your arms. You're a dolt, you can barely draw a circle, you're a wimp. What's happened serves you right. That'll teach you how big your boots are! What did it all add up to? Took yourself for an Antonello, did you? But you're barely good enough to make a proper *gesso duro*. We thought we were the greatest forger *auf der Erde*, did we? We thought it would be kind of fun to make a real period piece, a cute little Renaissance portrait, did we? So we said to ourselves why not let's have a go mate it's better than twiddling thumbs. Indeed it is. But a wee *Condottiere* can't be pinned down just like that. The other guy had been around for a while. He knew how things stacked up. Had a few tricks up his sleeve. But you're as witless as a day-old chick with cotton wool between its ears, and you've got no experience either. A nothingburger.

Something murky. What was murky? Something he still couldn't understand. A connection, a link. A link in the chain. Altenberg, Geneva, Split, Sarajevo, Belgrade. Then Paris. Then Rufus. Then

Madera? Meanwhile? The evening of the reception, or the day before, or the day after. At first, nothing. Nothing to report. Days dragged on. Then came facts, a story, a fate, a caricature of fate. To end with this obviousness, this bloody heap, Madera's corpse, and blood trickling between the feet of the chair . . .

Escape, of course, but why? What's in the way? Some plaster, some bricks, not much stone, and then some packed earth. How many feet? A man-sized hole, just beneath the level of the basement window. How many hours? The same image crosses your mind like a sudden and brutal slap: Rufus bursting into the studio to find you right here, slumped on your bed surrounded by cigarette butts, half hidden in a cloud of smoke . . . Otto had made a call. Was Rufus out? What would he be doing in his hotel room at four in the afternoon? Otto will call again this evening . . . You've still got a chance. A few hours . . . Enough time to get the right tools . . .

Wherever it may be, one day a telephone will crackle and a far distant voice will come through, there'll be the sound of footsteps, the knock on your door, three soft taps, there'll be a hand on your shoulder, somewhere, sometime, in the metro, on a beach, in the street, at a station. A day, a month, a year will have gone by, hundreds or thousands of miles will have been travelled, and someone will suddenly hail you, come up to you, will meet your gaze for an instant and then vanish. Night train. Empty compartment. Fuzzy images. You'll be lying on your bunk, no way out. Who will get you first – Rufus, or the police? One and then the other? A fine piece of melodrama, an avenging finger pointed at you – that's him we've got him keep it up lads go to it – then banner headlines in huge type. In court today. Read all about it. Eight columns wide. Headless corpse found in alley. You shall show my head to the people. Second by second. The carriage shudders over the fish-plates. Every sixty feet? Every thirty feet? You're fleeing. Fleeing at 120 kilometres an hour. You're in an empty train rushing along at 120 kilometres an hour. You're sitting in a facing seat by the window. Wan lights flicker now and then on the other side of the cold pane. Where are you going? Genoa, Rome, Munich. Anywhere. What are you running away from? The whole world knows you are on the run, you're standing still, the moon on the horizon is keeping up with you. Anywhere as long as it's out of this world. You won't make it.

He was cold. The cigarette he'd tossed on the floor was burning itself out. A wisp of smoke rose vertically almost to meet his eye, then broke into irregular whorls that wobbled for a few seconds and then dispersed as if blown by an invisible puff from nowhere, maybe a draught from the window.

Truth. Nothing but the. I killed Madera. I killed Anatole. I killed Anatole Madera. The killer of Anatole Madera was me. I did murder. Murdered Anatole Madera. Everyone murdered Madera. Madera is a man. Man is mortal. Madera is mortal. Madera is dead. Madera had to die. Madera was going to die. All I did was speed things up a bit. He was under sentence. He was ill. His doctor reckoned he had only a few years of life left. If you can call that a life. My word, did he live in pain. He wasn't feeling very well that afternoon. He had a lot on his mind. If I hadn't done anything maybe he would have died in any case. He would have gone out like a candle just by blowing himself out. He would have committed suicide . . .

"I don't think that'll be a problem." What did he know about it, in the first place, and why had he said it? The surroundings in that lounge, the potential effect of the lighting, the bar, the fire in the hearth. They both had a glass in their hands. And at a stroke the whole world, his whole world, materialised around him. After a long period of solitude the past suddenly became present, he was abruptly immersed in all that was most familiar to him, reduced to the dimensions of a lounge: everyone was there in the off-kilter lighting made of jagged leaps of reddish flames in the hearth and the excessively muted, over-intimate and artificial glow from the bar. Jérôme. Rufus and Juliette, Mila. Anna and Nicolas. And Geneviève. And Madera, supremely detestable, with teeth that gleamed when he smiled. Winter suit. A ballroom dancer's black-and-white shoes. At that point perhaps he should have been wary, should have thought calmly and methodically to try to understand what it all meant, what was henceforth impossible. He could see the full, stark, unaltered story of his last twelve years just by looking in those eight smiling faces. Coincidences or plots? Did he need to go beyond the smiles, further than twelve years back? To find a chink in the wall, a logical connection. An equation: there had been this, then there was that. To make the world coherent once again, or for the first time, a reassuring world, so much more reassuring than all this flux and vagueness. When was that? When was it supposed to be? Was it one evening in the abominable heat of Sarajevo, in loneliness all the more absurd for being accepted? An afternoon looking at the Condottiere? There would be a sign, and he could already see the complicated workings of a machine set in motion: a switch clicks, a needle points, a filament breaks, and valves open ... Would that do the trick? Had it done the trick? The oldest story in the world. His arm raised, the glint of a blade. Was that all it took for Madera to collapse with his throat slit?

Now I'm lying on this bed, I haven't shifted for maybe an hour. I'm not expecting anything. But I do want to live. Everybody wants to live. All the same I do maybe have enough time left to get up, get to work, dig a hole, and escape. Couldn't be easier. Couldn't be harder. What's difficult about it ...? Otto is now on the other side of the door and pacing up and down. He might have got through to Rufus, he might have told him ...

Might you be a coward? You are going to die. To die or tomorrow. You're going to die very slowly. From fear. Thou shalt rot. To be scraped off the floor with a teaspoon, swept up, vacuumed away and disposed of in the waste. You like that. It amuses you.

You'd like to look in the mirror and make faces. You'd like to wait until it's all over without lifting a finger, without doing a thing, you'd like it to be just a bad dream so you can rewind and go back a day, a month or a year. You wait. He hangs around outside your door. He's stupid and obedient, that's fine. Good dog. Guard dog. You could try to bribe him. You go up to the door and raise your voice. Herr Otto Schnabel, would you like to earn ten thousand dollars for nothing? My dear dear Otto, ten thousand dollars, all yours. Ten thousand dollars and three cents? Ten thousand times ten thousand. A billion dollars? A big pack of chewing gum. An alien outfit with all the accessories. A machine gun with dum-dum bullets. A stuffed elephant. Come on, Otto, show some willing. Make a gesture. You want an ottomobile. An ottomatic. A nelly copter. You want a nellycopter. Without propellors. A nellyjet.

You. You, the world's greatest art forger. The grinning joker, inside art. You think that's funny. You think waiting is a hoot. You've had enough, you're fed up with it. At the end of your tether. What about tomorrow? And the day after? And the day after that? And the day after the day after? You can't build the world from enlargements. You can't conquer the world with side-angle lighting. You can't lay out the world on a restored panel. You took a gamble and you lost. So what?

Aware of your own misery. And the runner-up is: Winckler, Gaspard, for his remarkable rendition of The Swan. Wearing gown, toga, and a crown of laurels, you grumble and grouse as you climb the four steps to the podium . . .

He stares at a blank spot on the wall. Tomorrow, tomorrow perhaps. Tomorrow dawn, or death. Or life. Or both, or neither, an intermediate state, a status quo. Why don't you drop in on me in my purgatory, the other side of no man's land . . .

Go looking. Go and look, of course. Look for light, for daylight on the other side. The other side of the mountain . . . The always fatal outcome of repetitious movements of the hand, the same skilfully adjusted dose of colour, the same trap set once again beyond overweening ambition? To strive for a *chef d'œuvre*. The ambition of Tintoretto and Titian resuscitated, risen from the ashes. Monumental ambition? Monumental mistake. *Antonellus Messaneus me pinxit.* Without the look, the certainty, or the confidence. A tin-pot portrait of a man. A mere princeling, a pasty-faced cad, a hairless and miserly coward. A Condottiere who'd taken the wrong turn, a miserable bit-part actor who'd not had time to learn his lines. And what about him? What was he doing mixed up in that – he, the one and only, the prince of forgers and forger of princes, with his fine nose and his eagle eye, his poison voice and magic hand. He who thought he could draw on the purest spring and summon from his ultra-modern easel the supreme quintessence of Italian art and the indisputable apogee of the Renaissance? Was he master of the universe? Meister Gaspard Winckler! Why shouldn't you laugh out loud? Señor Gaspard Winkleropoulos, alias El Greco. The world in his right hand. A walking art gallery!

You've killed a man, you have, don't you see. You committed murder. You think it's easy. Well, it's not. You think that committing murder has a meaning. Well, it doesn't. You think it's easy to paint a Condottiere. Well, it's not. Nothing is easy. Nothing is quick. Everything is wrong. You could not but get it wrong. You could only ever end up like this. Caught in your own trap, by your own folly, by your own lies . . .

*

My future all of a sudden is laid out before me in time and space. Just these few yards still to cross. Just these few hours still to get through. It all comes down to this. This is where it all comes to a halt, where it all comes to a stop. It's the edge and the threshold. It has to be crossed, and then anything can happen. The minute I get through the wall of this room maybe everything will begin to have a meaning again: my past, my present and my future. But first thousands upon thousands of meaningless gestures have to be performed one by one. Raise the arm, lower the arm. Until the earth shakes. Until the wall bursts and night shines forth in starry splendour. It's simple. The simplest thing in the world. Raise the arm, arm raised, like . . .

Gather your strength, try to summon it all up for a single push so as to begin living again, take this first step and be something other than a man lying on a bed playing at being dead in his own grave, the man you're staring at as if he were somebody else. Why is it so easy? Why is it so hard? You don't move. What's the point of having a conscience? You killed a man. That's serious. Very. Not a thing you should do. Madera hadn't hurt you. Why did you kill Madera? No motives. He was fat and alive, he puffed like a sea-lion, he was ugly, he was heavy, he wandered around the laboratory, dangerously, right behind you, saying nothing, not looking at you; he hovered around the easel with his hands behind his back and his lips slightly parted, wheezing from asthma; he would go away and slam the door and you could hear his steps echoing in the stairwell, under the arch, and for a long time after that as you got back to painting with slightly unsteady hands, feeling outraged without knowing why, almost in a panic from the presence of that man, that mass of breathless fat that prowled around for a few minutes and disappeared and then returned just as hostile and mistrustful, making you feel as flustered as a schoolboy who'd been caught out, caught red-handed, sitting too far back in your chair, your brush hanging idly in your hand and an absent look on your face, looking at that never-endingly unfinished portrait of another evil and aggressive visage as if it were the most obvious symbol of the whole adventure. Was that the reason why Madera died? Was that also the reason why you killed him?

Imprisoned, obviously. As in the Belgrade studio, long before. What was he waiting for in order to return? What was he really after? He had read Geneviève's letter. "It seems to me sometimes that I understand you completely, absolutely, from top to bottom. I have to say that's a pity, and also that I hope I'm wrong: if I am wrong then you must come back very quickly, as quickly as you can; if you put it off, then it can only mean I'm right, and you'd have to admit that everything that might have brought us together has lost all meaning." That last sentence had made his eyes prickle as he sought desperately, for the fourth, fifth and eighth time to tell Geneviève why he was not yet able to go back to Paris. He crossed out words, crumpled up the paper and threw it away, started again . . . "You have to wait three more days, because one of the specialists from the Commission has just discovered in the National Library in Sarajevo a virtually unknown manuscript about Roman remains in the lower part of Split, in close proximity to the site of the eastern wall of

Diocletian's Palace, which suggests very strongly that excavations were undertaken on the site in 1908 with no results, and that is very serious . . ."

Very serious. His eyes wandered desolately from one canvas to the other. Dear Geneviève. I cannot come back yet because. You'll have to wait another day or two. You have to carry on waiting because. He recalled that in that exact moment when the crossed-out words – the tiny, utterly futile sentences he could not manage to put together because the whole was just as meaningless as the parts – jumped out at him like a swarm of poisonous sea-lice, in that same exact moment when out of his too-empty studio came the implacable, ironical and fleeting image of a prison, that same moment when as the crumpled sheets piled up on the floor there came to him the painful awareness of a blatant deception – the discovery of that disastrous manuscript was a grotesque invention – at that exact same moment his gaze wandered beyond the wide-open window to a place four hundred metres away on the other side of Bezistan, beneath the friendly, warm-looking great red star of *Borba* that lit up the dark night, where the supposed consolation of a good booze-up awaited him in the press bar, the only place open so late. Could it be? Was it only now that this memory took on its full meaning, or had he been fully aware of it at the time? Had he deliberately agreed to seek refuge in a straightforward binge that would prevent him facing up to that letter for twelve hours or more? He'd picked up the phone, gone through his address book to find the right person to wake at 4.00 a.m. to go with him, lead him in his desperate quest for slivovitz, he'd found a suitable friend, an Italian journalist who might be at his hotel, he'd called the hotel . . .

His hands more than his memory recalled the movements that one by one, in apparently incorruptible and anonymous innocence had begun to dismantle, undermine and demolish the impressive construction of his sanctuary. 2-3-0-1-9 Hotel Moskva, someone gabbled. *Molim. Donnez-moi Mr Bartolomea Spolverini.* Please could you call up Mr Spolverini. *Bitte ich will sprechen zu Herr Spolverini.* Certainly, sir. Clunks and clicks. Ringing in the far distance, the sound of footsteps, orders given curtly. Certainly, sir. The far-off, spiteful voice pregnant with innocent danger. Waiting. Second by second. Kilometres of cable weaving all round the earth . . . Dear Geneviève. Dear Geneviève I? I am going to drink instead of packing and catching the plane. Full stop. Tomorrow he will be dead drunk lying fully dressed in an unmade bed among Streten's canvases, instead of being at Orly on a bright September day. Dear Geneviève. Paris, France. Waiting. Hands on the receiver, one of them gripping the earpiece, the other just touching it, held like a loudspeaker as if to mask the vileness of the conversation he was about to have, to hide the weakness under the words, the frankly excessive dismay, the self-confessed powerlessness, in all its tergiversation, to fabricate anything beyond a fictitious treasure . . . What's the point of being aware?

He didn't know much about real life. His fingers brought forth only ghosts. Maybe that was all he was good for. Age-old techniques that served no purpose, that referred only to themselves. Magic fingers. The relationship between the skills of a Roman jeweller, the knowledge of a Renaissance painter, the brush-stroke of an Impressionist and the patiently learned capacity to judge what substance to use, what preparation was required, what agility to develop – that relationship was merely a matter of technique. His fingers knew. His eyes took in the work, divined its fundamental dynamic, split it down to its tiniest elements, and translated them into what for him were internalised words such as a more or less liquid binding agent, a medium, a backing material. He worked like a well-oiled machine. He knew how to lead the eye astray. He had the art of combination. He had read da Vinci and Vasari and Ziloty and the *Libro dell'Arte*; he knew the rules of the Golden Ratio; he understood – and knew how to create – balance and internal coherence in a painting. He knew which brushes to use, which oils, which hues. He knew all the glazes, supports, additives, varnishes. So what? He was a first-class craftsman. Out of three paintings by Vermeer, van Meegeren could create a fourth. Dossena did the same with sculpture; Joni Icilio and Jérôme likewise. But that wasn't what he'd been after. From the Antonellos in Antwerp, London, Venice, Munich, Vienna, Paris,

Padua, Frankfurt, Bergamo. Genoa, Milan, Naples, Dresden, Florence and Berlin could have arisen with admirable obviousness a new Condottiere rescued from oblivion by an amazing find unearthed in some abandoned monastery or castle by Rufus, Nicolas, Madera or another one of their associates. But that wasn't what he wanted, was it?

What was the illusion he had cherished? That he would be able to cap an untarnished career by carrying off what no forger before him had dared attempt: to create an authentic masterwork of the past, to recover in palpable and tangible form, after a dozen years' intense labour, something far above the technical tricks and devices of his trade such as mere mastery of *gesso duro* or monochrome painting – to recover the explosive triumph, the perpetual *reconquista*, the overwhelming dynamism that was the Renaissance. Why was that what he'd been after? Why had he failed?

What remained was the feeling of an absurd undertaking. What remained was the bitterness of failure; what remained was a corpse. A life that had suddenly collapsed, and memories that were ghosts. What remained was a wrecked life, irreparable misunderstanding, a void, a desperate plea . . .

Now you're on your own and you're rotting in your cellar. You're cold. You can't make sense of it anymore. You've no idea what happened. You've no idea how it happened. But the one who's alive is you, here, in this same place, you at the end of twelve years of a featureless existence, an existence pregnant with nothing. Every month, every year you dumped your packet of masterpieces. And then? Then nothing ... And then Madera died ...

Arm raised, the glint of the blade. All it took was a gesture. But first he had had to get the razor out of its sheath, check its condition, fold it in his palm so he could use it, leave the laboratory, climb the stairs one by one. One after another. Slowly. At each step the aim became more precise. What was he thinking about? Why was he thinking? He was perfectly aware: he was climbing the stairs to go and slit Anatole's throat, the throat of the late Anatole Madera. The thick fat throat of Anatole Madera. His left hand would be wide open to provide a better grip as he applied it firmly and speedily to the forehead and pulled it backwards, and his right hand would slit the man's throat with a single thrust. Blood would spurt. Madera would collapse. Madera would be dead.

He had done all those things. First in the half-light each hand had put a glove on its partner, rubber gloves similar to medical ones, which he sometimes used when working clay. He had done all that. Step by step. One two three. Four. Five six. With frequent stops. To get his breath back. To wait. And all that while – what was the point? – a voice spoke to him from the back of his neck, from his head, from his big toe. It never stopped talking. Step by step. Seven eight nine ten. Let it go again. What was his conscience going on about? What was his guardian angel rattling on about? Gordian angel. Step by step. Come on lad don't let it get you down. You're right you're wrong. Freedom or death. Tread by tread. Step by step. Rather be the slicer than the slice. Step by step. One step for Ma. One step for De. One step for Ra. One step for You. One step for Shall. One step for

Kill one step for Ma one step for De one step for Ra. You Shall Kill Ma De Ra. You shall kill Madera. Ma De Ra. Almost as if neon signs were going on inside his head, flashing then vanishing, and, as if as he gradually drew nearer to his goal, the oak door, the padded door, the door ajar on whose other side everything would begin and end just as it had all begun and ended when a year and half before behind that same door the little Christ by Bernardino dei Conti had emerged from an unsuspected drawer, as if the entire set-up that he had glimpsed for a few seconds had now come back to him in its fear, anxiety, anger, despair, greed, boldness, courage, madness, and certainty, as if all of that had coalesced and was fleeing at phenomenal speed towards that thick, red neck with its fleshy folds touching the white silk shirt that like an irresistible magnet invited, demanded the unspeakable gesture, the incision of the glinting blade that would set off a pulsing cataract of blood and with it the chaos of a revolt that had been kept hidden for too long.

No, there had been nothing to it. Just one dead man. Beyond a forced smile, an arbitrary tensing of the jaw, a hat out of kilter. Beyond a maybe poorly inspired brooch in the strict organisation of the painting: the inaccessible and terrifying Mr Condottiere had hovered over that paltry anxiety . . .

Over there and far away, the recovered delirium is once again seething. Seething thickly on the terra firma of certainties. Dura mater, pia mater. Arachnoid. Did his conscience remember in order to protect itself? Gaspard the forger. What sense was there in his crazy desire to jump over the inevitable flowing river of time to recreate the radiant mug – yellow and translucent, like a good candle – of that ruffian? But it was all logical; it seemed that some particular event had intervened at every moment in his life to undermine the false calm he had thought he enjoyed day by day: meeting Mila had trained him for unhappiness; meeting Geneviève had built the walls of his prison; the death of Madera was the final conclusion, the obvious and necessary apotheosis. Where was the surprise? He had been trapped. To paint the look in the eyes of a condottiere, he would have had to look in the same direction as he had, if only for an instant. It was so obvious that what had attracted him had been this immediate image of triumph, the complete opposite of what he was himself! Even his most Herculean labours could not prevent what had to be from coming into being: in the shadow of the Condottiere, all he could attain was the image of his own failure.

What did it matter, anyway? There's nothing for you to face up to yet. Death, if you will, but death doesn't mean much in the end. What you have behind you is this muddled story, your own story: the story of an idiot, to put it bluntly, not without a modicum of sensitivity, not devoid of a love of fine things, not entirely lacking in taste – but an idiot nonetheless. Behind you lies Madera's corpse, an impressive number of more or less serious failures, a kind of disillusionment, and a few hundred successes you can't claim as your own because you took great pains to ascribe them to other artists. Behind you are masks. In you there is nothing. A desire to carry on living. A wish to die. A feeling of emptiness and an arrant failure to understand. So what?

Everything you do has a price, you should know that. You should have picked that up, to your own cost. Every word you utter, every thought you turn over in your mind has a necessary consequence. Nothing comes for free. Everything has to be paid for and the cost is often high. Laughter, mockery, messing up won't get you anywhere. You still have to get up and look around and stop this stupid game. What have you got to lose? What's at stake? Another hour will go by. Then twelve. The door will be knocked down. That's what you're pondering in your little head. The door will be knocked down. They'll come and get you. They'll take you to prison. You're not scared. You can easily envisage a cell not so different from the one you're in, only maybe a bit smaller. With a harder bed, darker walls. Some graffiti, to while away the time. Dates, or notches, or grids to mark the days? . . . Robinson Crusoe's calendar. 34,089 in clink, or something of that kind. And then?

Would you like to go on living? Say yes. Yes, and yes again. The pleasure of walking in the sun, the pleasure of walking in the rain, the pleasure of travelling, of eating. And swimming. Hearing the sound of a train? All you have to do is dig for a few metres. Earth and sod, brick and stone, cement and plaster. You'll be able to unlodge a stone. Will you manage to avoid Otto, to slip noiselessly through the lawns in the grounds, to get through the electric fence? Will you manage to get back on the road? You can flee in life, you can flee in death. And then? You're making a bet . . .

He looks at his watch. Murky light seeps through the ivy-cluttered basement window. Millions and millions of kilometres weaving all around the planet. Heads or tails. He gets up. He strides around the laboratory. Where is the chink, the invisible pivot? Open Sesame? Which stone will swing open? He glances all round the room. There'll be a narrow passage, dripping corridors, stairs, steel ladders, a whole underground route stretching out for miles, a labyrinth of dark passageways, a knot of abandoned cuttings, a long march strewn with obstacles and countless side-tracks marked by tiny signs, leading, beyond the mines and quarries, to the trans-figured reality of a clearing in the woods, to the marvellous presence of a rain-drenched night, to the discovery of an intense and radiant sky.

Scrap by scrap. His chisel grazes the mortar: a sharp, accurate blow from his hammer and a shard of cement flies off from the dense layer surrounding each block of masonry. At each effort, each blow, the way out begins to open, the route becomes clearer, an exit looms, still far away but nonetheless present . . .

With every inch you dig out you question the world. Why and for whom are you fighting? What hope do you still have? You think you understand. You think you know. But what next? How will you live tomorrow? In a few hours you will be free and you know it; the mere repetition of the same movement will save you: you aim your chisel, raise your arm, bring it down, do it again. And then?

Perhaps you will dig down into your life just as you are digging your way to salvation? Go back to square one and start again. Understand. Two or three times in the course of your life it was necessary for you to make a choice, and you probably made the wrong one, and now it is perhaps possible for you to avoid making mistakes about yourself, not to repent but to accept yourself, to concentrate on only the essential facts, to rub out . . . With stylet, scalpel, graving tool or indeed a chisel . . . Scrape, thrust, up-end . . . Get rid of and blank out what had been, what had been lousy, what had been wrecked and ruined. Shattered. Stitch by stitch, step by step, undo everything he had done, everything he had believed . . . And then repeat the movement for ever more, start over again and again: set the chisel in place, hit it with the hammer, even if it seemed pointless and absurd, even if he ended up not knowing what he was digging for.

In a few hours he would be out. And then? He would avoid Otto, he would kill him if necessary, he would tidy himself up a bit, then go on to the road and stop a car or a lorry. He would get back to Paris. And then?

This is where everything stops and everything begins. The swing of the arm is so simple. In two or three hours the loosened stones would swing round, crash onto your trestle, roll onto the cement floor. All you'll have to deal with then is a layer of compacted soil. In four hours. In time and space your future is suddenly inscribed . . .

That resistance. That peculiar resistance of the world and yourself. Like in Altenberg, long ago. That fresh snow that had frozen over. Like corrugated iron. He was walking on an empty slope with his skis on his shoulder; the snow seemed able to bear his weight, it stood up to him, then suddenly collapsed, and he sank into it up to his thighs. He'd barely been able to put on his skis and go back down, very fast. He slid along, barely touching the ground, he managed not to get lost and not to fall in. It was an odd memory. Wasn't it the case that all he had done for years was to glide over the surface of things? That resistance, that simulacrum of resistance. He had never gone any further. Not for Rufus, not for Geneviève, not for Jérôme. Not for anybody. Not even for himself. Were they alive? Were they anything other than nameless, rootless, and unmoored beings? As if he had been living in a wandering world. A world of ghosts. And yet, on some occasions, on the evening of the party, which he felt all of a sudden like a fearsome threat, as if he'd been abruptly summoned to appear in court, taken apart and stripped bare without mercy and then pinned to the wall, he had felt splashed by the existence of other people, with fear and then an understanding that was immediate, intuitive, spontaneous and irrefutable. That sharp burst of their existence. Maybe that crust on the snow that was hard only on the surface was cracking and collapsing – beneath what weight? – and was dragging him down, invading him . . . That was such a long way from the well-guarded, closed world he had set about building, his citadel of stucco and imitation marble, his strictly limited empire of the ersatz, the home of useless alchemical tricks.

His hands could bring Vermeer or Pisanello back to life, just as he could revive Greek craftsmen, Roman goldsmiths, Celtic coppersmiths, or Kyrgys silversmiths. But so what? People said bravo, they looked after him, paid him, congratulated him, treated him like a star. And then? What remained? What had he done? What you did at Split . . .

In a cellar in the lower town a treasure hoard was born: earthenware and sandstone pots, vats and amphoras stuffed full of jewels and coins, sesterces, silver denarii, bracelets, pins, cameos, huge silver brooches, all higgledy-piggledy and deeply buried – a disparate, extravagant hoard that matched quite miraculously what might well have been the treasure-chest of a lord of the Late Empire, a high dignitary of the state stuck in this far-away province that was still Roman but already invaded by barbarians, if only in the mixed origins of the people in his entourage, who one day had been expelled with his followers from the palace by yet another invasion and pursued in an endless retreat towards Styria, or Illyria, or Gallia Cisalpina or else towards the east, up-river, towards Macedonia or the Carpathians, leaving people and goods where they were, and, in a constantly nurtured hope of returning, hiding in a cellar an impressive mound of gold, silver, and precious stones that formed the unambiguous insignia of a thousand years' domination . . .

And then? Had he been aware that what he had been seeking once again was his own image? Had he known that what he had summoned up, what he had snatched out of the past, what he had projected onto the four dripping, damp, dark walls of the cellar in Split was his own face, his own attitude, his own ambiguity? A treasure was hidden inside. A year of painstaking research, months of solitary labour. A few hundred metres from the bluest sea in the world, with his tiny forge, his gold and silver leaf, his unsorted precious stones, his wooden and brass mallets, working in an untanned leather apron just as, long before, a slave-smith had worked, a man who might have been a cowherd from Transylvania or a Greek shepherd, a tiny dot in a mile-long horde, driven by cold or hunger, or by wolves that had been attracted from their lairs in Latvia or Cappadocia by the Empire's alleged garden of Eden, the great ship of peace reigning over the world and by the unbounded horizon of Mare Nostrum but which nonetheless was ineluctably peeling away and caving in under the sheer weight of its own coherence – this cowherd or shepherd, dragged against his will into a useless adventure, by sudden turns horseman, foot-soldier, prisoner of war, and slave, extracting from iron, bronze and gold not just the angry pride of freedom lost, but the unspoken longing for the glimpse he had had of peace.

But what had come of his own effort, of his slow and blinkered striving, his indefatigable energy, the four months he had spent in a cellar working twelve to fifteen hours a day? What reassurance? What certainty? He had worked in torrid heat, almost naked but for his apron, surrounded by a never-ending swarm of flies, leaving his workbench only when darkness fell, not seeing a soul apart from a vague acquaintance of Nicolas who brought him his food twice a day. Why and for whom had he slaved away? Geneviève had asked him not to leave, he had refused; later, she asked him to come back, and he had refused again. Was his love no stronger than that? He had obstinately tried to convince her, claiming in complete bad faith that it was just a question of a week or two, seeing all the work he'd put in, the paperwork that had been assembled, the money that had been put up, the negotiations that Nicolas and Rufus were conducting . . .

And now you're digging crumb by crumb. Unpredictable geometry of the rock being tackled. No order, no logic: just the continuity of the hammering you're giving it. Your arm hurts. Your head is buzzing. Do you want to go on? Why do you ask? You mustn't stop. You'll collapse from fatigue, your chisel will slip from your hand, you won't hit hard enough. You have to exhaust yourself. Like an animal. You must not pause to recover. Don't ask any more questions. Or else don't answer them. Why is that suddenly reassuring? The width of the chisel, the accuracy of your hammering, those shards cluttering up the plank and the trestle, those stones which are coming apart, millimetre by millimetre. In a few hours you'll be sliding through the wet grass like a worm. Shirtless, shoeless, kneeling at the top of the scaffolding with your head almost touching the ceiling, bathed in sweat, you hammer away like a deaf man on the rough, off-white surface of the mortar and each blow echoes inside you with a long-drawn-out, strident intensity, with an obsessive rhythm . . .

Months and months, all that pointless effort? As if he had such powerfully rooted habits, or rather, a stubborn wish to go on; whatever the cost, to go to the very limits of his own misery, his own weakness. A decision taken once and for all to be entirely and only that absence, that hollow, that mould, the duplicator, false creator and mechanical agent of works of the past. Those clever hands, that precise knowledge of what erosion means to paint, his skill and craft. What did he want? Guilty or not guilty . . .

Sometimes, in spite of himself, his hands, his neck, shoulders and ankles shook, seized up, got cramp. He pressed on with clenched teeth, sometimes making a rough whistling sound, absorbed in his struggle, as if he were no longer capable of stopping, as if all his life had migrated to the flat, shiny blade of the chisel with which he was pummelling the mortar like a machine, had migrated into his painful, overdone, ever more tense movements and which with every second, with every minute, were loosening, unfixing the stone that would become a new door open onto the night.

The bedazzlement of life. From deep down in his consciousness rise the snows of Altenberg, the banners floating over the Olympic piste, the huzzahs of the crowd. And then the same fatigue and that feeling of peace. How beautiful he found those first steps towards conquest, the horizon suddenly coming into view after a long night's march. A small party of four or five men, barely a rope. Sunrise near the top of the Jungfrau. The suddenly revealed view of the Alps, on the other side of the mountain. The watershed. As if it had all hung on the suddenly friendly and familiar presence of the sun. Near. Because it was cold or because they'd had to walk a long way to see it? Because his climb had been nothing more than the desperate call of that radiance . . .

Why not understand? And why should he have forgotten? Then one by one the masks had come: meeting Jérôme, getting settled in Geneva. An absurd memory. Altenberg and its too fresh snow, a thousand slivers of light, the proud accumulation of layers beneath the apparent protection of the iced-over surface that glinted in the sunlight. Altenberg, whose traces lay in him like ski-tracks: parallel headlong lines accompanied by a quincunx pattern of roundels, slightly inclined towards the direction of travel, made by ski-sticks scraping their steel tips visibly if minutely, and more or less deeply, on the snow.

Those vanishing, intertwining tracks, still sharp or else half rubbed out, each of which compacted the snow, solidified the ground, made it less and less fragile, less and less deceptive, just as – in the present – memories rose up in him, intertwined and vanished, strengthening his approach, and, like those pistes that were too hard for him to tackle, leaving immaculate, hostile landscapes of virgin snow on the north slope, offering wide open spaces that were waiting for him. Every instant, now, beyond the snow, beyond his memories, the paltry image of his own death rose up, the image of his fate, of his ridiculous saga, and the sickening grimaces of the masks. Twenty years had gone by. A hundred forged paintings, or more . . .

And here you are, at the present time, with your life in your hands, wallowing neck-high in your own story, and more lost in your memories than you ever were before. A tear wells up, you're so touched by your own weakness. But you know very well that things did not happen like that. What's the use of complaining? You wanted to be what you were. You were what you wanted to be. You accepted your fate, whole and entire, not because you were obliged to accept something, not as a victim, but definitely because the way you structured your life, your work, your entertainment, remained the most likely way to provide you with satisfaction. It was you who followed Jérôme, it wasn't Jérôme who led you astray . . .

But what difference did that make today? Yes, it had all been messed up. Yes, he had messed it all up. He had accepted the world in its easiest manifestation. He had intended to lie. He had lied. He had made lying his business. And then? He had wanted to run away and it was too late . . .

At an altitude of three thousand metres between Belgrade and Paris, maybe over Basel or Zurich, perhaps above Altenberg, the salutary decision he had mulled over for too long had at last been made to have done with forgeries and go away with Geneviève. They would have gone to the Balearics first, then to the United States. He would have earned a living as a restorer. But he had not alerted Geneviève . . . He had not answered her last letter, which he had had for ten days. When the plane made a stop at Geneva, he had sent a telegram. But when he reached Orly, only Rufus and Juliette were waiting for him, and they took him back to their place where there was a cocktail party going on, where he had hooked up with Jérôme. Then with Anna, Mila and Nicolas. Then Madera. Then Geneviève . . .

She had left straight away. He hadn't spoken to her. Had Gaspard been nailed or screwed to the floor? He had not seen her since. Sixteen or eighteen months later, that telephone call, in the middle of the night . . .

She had not answered. She must have woken up with a start. Then understood. Who could be calling her at that hour? Then waited. Then decided quite quickly that she would not get up, that she would not pick up, and then she must have listened, maybe counting the rings, and got up all the same, then hesitated, switched the lights on, edged closer to the telephone, hesitated again, mesmerised by the ringing, hesitated yet again, then put out her arm, brought her hand towards the receiver, unable to decide whether to pick up or cut the caller off . . . Perhaps he had not waited long enough, perhaps he'd let himself get swallowed up by the regular sequence of rings, as if each of them merely emphasised the futility of this final attempt. Ring. Silence. Those tinny crackles on the line, over there, on the other side of Paris, here, right in his ear. How his patience and pointless obstinacy must have reassured her . . . Sometimes I feel I understand you, completely, inside out . . . What would have happened if she had picked up, if she had answered, if she had agreed to see him again? How long would it have been until he went back to Dampierre? Was he free? Was he a prisoner?

Sixteen or eighteen months later, at night, that telephone call. That crazy call. That automatic, almost automatic gesture, like so many others after all, following on from those dozens and dozens of numbers, dozens and dozens of letters on the dial. Counted out one by one. Always with that same anxiety. And the same impatient desire for a dialogue wrested from space, recreating, in a bizarre coherence, that universe of wires and networked lines, those thousands of faithful and impassive operators in headsets, those kilometres of cable weaving all round the globe, not so much in his mind the eternal muttering of time and history as the soothing web of a potential release, simply connected to the refusal or the acceptance of one's self, of one's fate, of one's destiny, the last bastion of one's freedom, those simple movements taken on board one by one, corresponding, beyond the electronic precision of the combined circuitry, to what could have been his definitive, immediate, indisputable victory over the world . . . B–A–B–1–5–6–3 – Everything became possible again, for the second time, one more time, beyond the clumsiness of the action, simply because at Rue d'Assas Geneviève had woken up, Geneviève had heard. But she was not the person he should have called.

He had driven from Gstaad to Lausanne then flew in a taxi-plane from Lausanne to Paris, and another taxi from Orly to Avenue de Lamballe. He had arrived at three in the morning. He had put his case in the hall. He had taken off his coat. He had gone up to the telephone. He had wanted to call Rufus first to explain why he'd left. Then Madera, to say that he was not going to go on, that he didn't want to be a forger anymore. But the number he had dialled – why? – was Geneviève's . . .

Was it really for her sake that you left Gstaad? Answer, no lying now: what were you after? You waited a long time. At each unanswered ring the world collapsed anew. Whole continents smashed to smithereens. Torrents of lava. Tidal waves. What was left? She had not answered. You hung up. You took off your jacket. You loosened your necktie. You looked at the time. You went to the kitchen. You drank a glass of water . . . You lay down, you woke up, you called Rufus in Gstaad. You got dressed . . .

He had taken a taxi to Gare Montparnasse. Another taxi from Dreux to Dampierre. Otto had opened the door, and he had not looked surprised. Madera had seen him in his study. He had told the older man that he'd had enough rest and had come back to finish the *Portrait of a Man*, and that he would have it completed in a week. He had gone down to the laboratory. He had taken off the piece of canvas that protected the panel. He had looked at the Condottiere . . .

You did all of those things, you lived all of those moments. Do you remember? That was three days ago. Everything was possible, you remember, you wanted it. You were waiting and at each ring

forger? How a forger? Since when a forger? He hadn't always been a forger . . .

Becalmed. Day in day out. Then the hours that started ticking away, putting their full weight on him. And then those deeds, those events, that adventure, story, fate – a caricature of a fate. A useless gesture, or a step in the right direction? In its unspeakable spontaneity, Madera's death was perhaps the first action of the demiurge emerging from chaos.

Night is falling. Rufus has not come. You're in with a chance. You just have to keep out of Otto's way. Otto is an idiot. Your arm hurts. Doesn't matter, keep going, the blocks are more than halfway to coming loose. You've had enough. I know. Who cares. Tell yourself it's exercise. Some kind of a match. A time-trial. Tell yourself you're carving a bas-relief. Tell yourself you'd be better off anywhere except this cellar. You're not convinced. Who cares. One more time who cares. You mustn't say who cares. Never look a gift-horse. It takes two Constables to catch a Whistler. Remember, that's your motto. Don't give up now. You're too close to the finish. Even so: you could carry on, or you could wait. Right? You try to overcome your own opposition. Of course you won't. Sure you will. I know you. You know yourself. Nonetheless. How many times have you hit the chisel with the hammer? A hundred thousand times? A million? Two hundred and fifty? You don't know? That's a good sign ... Listen here: you and me pal, we're gonna do a bunk, right? Jump the fence? That'll give Rufus a nasty surprise ...

To die not to die. What did that mean, free or not free, guilty or not guilty? What would that so strictly, so definitively disastrous arc look like such that he would end up being able to describe it? Madera was dead. Why? What was the more important? Where had it all started? The party at Rufus's place? The night at the studio in Belgrade? The sudden return from Gstaad? Meeting Jérôme? Meeting Mila? Meeting Geneviève? Or was it the night he had spent drinking in this very basement? What was left of his whole life? Where had it begun? What was the logic?

Gaspard Winckler, trained at the École du Louvre, holding a diploma in Painting Conservation from New York University and the Metropolitan Museum, New York, Honorary Technical Consultant at the Musée des Beaux-Arts, Geneva, restoration expert at the Koenig Gallery, Geneva. So what? A notorious counterfeiter in his spare time. A forger more than he should have been. So what? He had been born, grown up and become a forger. How can you be a forger? You are the forger . . . Why become a forger? Did he need money? No. Had he been blackmailed? Hardly. Did he like it? So-so.

So hard to explain. At the time, could he have imagined anything else? He was walking the streets of Berne. It was wartime. He was seventeen. Idle and wealthy. And Jérôme arose. The attraction of mystery. An adventure. A clever and elegant Arsène Lupin. On his endless vacation, surrounded by extremely wealthy old ladies from England, canny hotel-keepers and retired diplomats, amidst postcard-pretty scenery – snow, mountain peaks, fine chocolate and high-class cigarettes – what could be better than that infallible painter? I'm a painter too but that's very good my lad. And then? The sudden discovery of something difficult. The sudden awareness that he had never known anything, that he had never understood what the act of painting meant, that he had only been making desultory use of a fairly good "hand" to keep boredom at bay, and the certainty that he could learn and become knowledgeable, one day. By immersing himself entirely in study and research, under Jérôme's patient but firm supervision. And then? Then by copying, pasticing, copying, imitating, reproducing, tracing, dissecting, five times, ten times a hundred times, every detail of Metsys's *Banker and his Wife*: mirror, books, coins, scales, box, hats, faces, hands. And then ...

Too good to be true, too easy. When did the whole business start to wobble? When did your story come unstuck? So, so irresponsible ... I was seventeen, of course. But when I was twenty-five, twenty-seven, thirty, thirty-three? Could he get his mind round it? What is the point of having a conscience? What's awareness for? It's a word. A word like any other. Conscious of what? The walls of the prison closed in on him at speed. Nothing more to say. One fake. Another fake. Gaspard the forger ...

Then came Mila. First bedazzlement. First slight, small and harmless. Simulated remorse. A tiny misunderstanding. For the first time in his life he had a sudden urge, just like that, to stop playing a game. To be himself. What did that mean? A rut is a rut. Gaspard the forger. Gaspard Winckler, supplier of a full range of forgeries. Anything by anybody of any period ...

Loving a woman, was that being himself? Did he love her? For many years love had meant using confidential visiting cards that Rufus gave him (he got them from Madera, but he only knew about that much later on). Anonymous encounters. And that was that. A need for slightly more spontaneous affection, for something rather less mechanical, a little less sordid. It was of no consequence. That was the way it was. He had met Mila at Nicolas's place. She'd become his mistress. Because of the colour of the dress she was wearing that day, or else because she had begun to smile. He could not remember. What did it matter? It was something like an interval. A few nights that were different from the others. The morning after, with pitiless logic, with pitiless idiocy, there he was at the Louvre, at the same time as always, in the Roman Antiquities section, with Nicolas, preparing the Hoard of Split. It spoke for itself. It had not even occurred to him that, without it making the slightest difference to anything, he could perfectly easily have given himself a week off. Was that natural? Guilty or not guilty . . .

When he had come into the room she was already there, seated on the arm of an enormous armchair close up to the fireplace, leaning slightly forward, talking to Jérôme. It was fairly odd. It had never occurred to him that she might know Jérôme. She turned to look at him, said nothing, didn't even smile or nod. He went a little closer. She stood up very naturally, and went to the other end of the room, where the bar was. A neutral attitude? Or was her indifference carefully calculated? What difference could it make? Doesn't matter. Things like that happen to everyone. You didn't love her, that's all. Or she didn't love you. But that's not the issue. Why did you feel guilty for a few seconds or minutes or days? You were indifferent. You didn't make the slightest effort. You would have liked to make an effort . . .

Strange. You think you're free. Then, at a stroke . . . No. Where did freedom begin? Where did it end? Free to fake? What an oddity.

A little Giottino. The Adoration of the Magi. Melchior, Balthazar. Gaspard. Have another go. And so it goes on. And it soon becomes essential, and there's nothing in the world besides that persistence and that patience, that obsession with exactness in respect of anything. Cézanne. Gauguin. The world recedes . . . And there he is already pinned up on the wall: Gaspard Winckler the Forger. Pinned down like a butterfly. Gasparus Wincklerianus. Wholly, fundamentally, explicitly, absolutely and completely defined. Sometimes I feel I understand you, completely, inside out . . . A forger, and what else besides? Just a forger. Joni Icilio the Forger, Jérôme Quentin the Forger, Gaspard Winckler the Forger. The forger with his auger. The drill of death, and passing time.

Time goes on and the masonry wobbles. In a few minutes this block – and the whole world around it, the world attached to it – will pivot and open the way. What about Rufus? Can you see him at the wheel of his Porsche screaming down the road, piercing the sky with his headlamps, the needle hovering around 120? Rufus worried, agitated, devastated . . .

One more try. And then? Your future written in stone. You'll never be a forger again. The one sure thing you require. You may live happily or unhappily, you may be rich or poor. Who cares. The world on your plate tomorrow? Just that one promise, never to lose yourself again, never to be taken in by your own game. Will you be able to keep the promise? Are you keeping it right now?

You've no idea. You don't yet have an idea. You've never been alive. Your hands and your eyes. The slave-smith, the Kyrgyz or

Visigoth coppersmith in his cowherd's apron. Your hands summon forth a forgotten caravan. You are dying in the midst of sightless corpses – the empty, bulging eyes of Roman statues – amidst masterpieces and trinkets, masked shamans waving painted fetishes and the resurrected enigmas of medieval sculpture. Look at them, they're all there, they're crowding in on you: El Greco, Caravaggio, Memling, Antonello. Silently, untouchably, inaccessibly, they are dancing all around you . . .

Yes. Jérôme as well, long ago. Alone and forgotten in his little house outside Annemasse. Died of hunger or loneliness among his art books and canvases. Died on a November day. He had not seen him for more than six months. He had paid him only one brief and shameful visit, not knowing what to say, scared and in a panic at the sight of his rapid decline, his foreseeable decline, at the suddenly intolerable sight of his trembling hands and the atrocious punishment of poor sight. Jérôme was unable to work anymore. He took slow steps around his untended garden, he wandered around his still-empty living room, twiddling his thick metal-framed glasses, which in his time of glory he would only wear to inspect a detail, claiming with a degree of pride that he only used them as a magnifying glass, and which made him look like Chardin but which he now had to wear almost permanently, changing their position on his nose to glance at a book he obviously knew already, and which like all his books dealt exclusively with the aesthetics or the techniques of painting, and he would then shut it again immediately, as if such subjects had become taboo, as if everything that by force of habit had been his whole life no longer existed, and could only set off a bout of searing nostalgia that he constantly denied and yet just as constantly rekindled with fear and trembling in the awful, futile illusion of recovery.

His wrinkled and calloused hands lay on the arm of the chair and sometimes shook a little. He would tense them abruptly, digging his nails into the upholstery. "I am very glad to see you, Gaspard. It's been quite a time, hasn't it?" The banality of the expression, its indifference, the mechanical way it was said. It was in Paris, the night of the party, his last time in Paris. And also the last time he'd spoken to him. Rufus was leaving next morning for Geneva and would drop him off at Annemasse . . .

Now he loitered on the streets and in the empty rooms of his villa. He was sixty-two. He looked eighty. He had been a pupil of Joni Icilio. He had had a truly distinguished career. One da Vinci, seven Van Goghs, two Rubens, two Goyas, two Rembrandts and two Bellinis. Fifty-odd Corots, a dozen Renoirs, thirty or more Degas, exported in bulk to South America and Australia in 1930 and 1940, a number of Metsys and Memlings and whole cartloads of Sisleys and Jongkinds, done between 1920 and 1925 at the start of his association with Rufus and Madera. Until 1955 he had worked twelve hours a day and often more, accumulating knowledge, techniques and tricks of the trade, and with every artist achieving indisputable perfection, often with startling speed. Then he had stopped and hung around Place du Cirque, giving advice, setting things up, making bibliographies, collecting documentation, as if he were still trying at whatever cost to make himself useful, and gradually, without saying anything at first, stopping completely, and as if he could not envisage carrying on living in idleness while remaining in the very place where he had spent his working life, confessing to Rufus (who had not dared bring up the subject himself) that he wished "to end his days" in peace and quiet, and so settled with obviously simulated delight and a sad little smile on his face in the detached house that Rufus had bought him at Annemasse, only a few hundred metres from the gates of Geneva, and there, with a sour housekeeper, a decent pension and a precious library, begun to experience the appallingly slow agony of living a life that was no longer any use. Two years. Seven hundred and thirty days. Seven hundred and thirty days of boredom only too rarely relieved by a visitor or a trip. A few days in Paris, Venice or Florence, and then he was on his own once again, alone with his oddly gentle pain, a kind of vaguely nostalgic, vaguely anaesthetising comprehension of the self, among his books and paintings, alone in his sparsely furnished living room and, beyond that, a small street lined with identical houses, a silent and empty little street. All his life he had lived in the ceaseless jostle of Rue Rousseau and Place du Cirque or else in Paris, in Rue Cadet, in a small studio on the seventh floor of a block of apartments. A livid, scrawny little street. A clean little suburban street? A cramped living room that he had not summoned up the courage to organise, as if he had been convinced that it was not worth the trouble, as if he had wanted to prove every minute of the day that he was already dead and living in his grave, in these alien and altogether unknown and indifferent surroundings where he was obliged nonetheless to walk and look and see every day . . .

On 17 November 1958, Rufus had called Dampierre: Jérôme was dying. That same evening, Otto drove him to Orly and he landed in Geneva. There was a chilly drizzle. When they reached Annemasse Jérôme was already dead. A doctor and the housekeeper were standing by his bed. An extraordinary jumble of open books, reproductions and unfolded lithographs was strewn around the bedroom, surrounding him like battle colours . . .

Do you recall? You bent down and picked up a book that had fallen close by Jérôme. Do you recall? *Let four captains bear Hamlet, like a soldier, to the stage; . . . and, for his passage, the soldiers' music and the rites of war speak loudly for him . . .*

The funeral march echoes for a long time in the burdened memory. Jérôme had wandered around the corridors of his house, going from room to room like a shadow, resting his head against the windows, staring at the narrow street. That was in November. A fine drizzle was falling. He paced back and forth, went up to his bookcase, opened his portfolios, took out thousands of sketches, removed the protective tissue paper from the prints, remembering, resuscitating each story, each detail, each one of the difficulties he'd faced and overcome. Then what?

He must have walked for a long time in the stunted little garden. Dusk had fallen. It was cold. He had gone back up to his room. He had gone back down to the living room. The housekeeper had served his dinner. He had not touched it. He had pushed his plate away with a gesture of great weariness . . .

Do you recall? You left for Paris the following morning. You came back here. Jérôme was dead. He was your master. He was a forger. You were a forger and you would die as well. One day you too would rot away in a deserted house. You went down to the laboratory. Here. You drew back the canvas drape protecting the Condottiere. You'd been working on it for a year . . .

Then one day you started drinking, straight from the bottle. Madera found you in the small hours, dead drunk and half strangled by your necktie. He said nothing. He did not ask any questions. He called Rufus on the telephone. Rufus came to get you. He took you to Gstaad. You spent three days with him and went skiing. You remembered Altenberg. But you couldn't even remember what had made you so happy. You got back to Paris in the middle of the night. You called Geneviève. She didn't answer. You went back to Dampierre . . . That was three days ago.

A few more blows of the hammer. Five four three. Two? One. Five more. Cuckoo! Watch the little birdie. Open Sesame. Over and out. Solemn Overture. Music by Johann Sebastian Bach. Fugue. One more go, with a bit more energy, and bingo, you've caught the ashlar like it was just a rugby ball. So that's that. Take a breather? You wipe your hands like a true stonemason. One stone. Another stone. And now. A hole in the wall. There's a bit of earth in front of you, all dirty and grey. The tiniest trickle of dusky light. Very poetic. But that doesn't mean you aren't in a right mess. No point in thinking Otto has gone back to his usual routine, or that by some miracle he's suddenly become as deaf as a doorpost. Therefore he has heard you. Therefore he knows roughly where the tunnel is. He is out there. If you stick your neck out you'll see him right in front of you. He'll tell you very sweetly, "Meester Gazpa, get ze fock pack in ze lap." So your tunnywunnel is useless. You don't give a damn. You'll find another way out. One way or t'other . . .

You get off your pedestal. You walk around the laboratory. Otto, my Otto, where art thou? Do you not see Milord Koenig coming down the lane? Did you get through to the aforementioned Switzerman? Did he tell you he would be with you forthwith? Are you expecting him at this very instant?

Very funny. Side-splitting. You look at your watch. It's a quarter to seven. There's still no reason why Rufus should be at his hotel at this time. Otto must have left a message . . . All you can do is carry on with your gamble. If Otto is on his own when you are completely ready to emerge, then you should be able to get away with it. For instance, if he's waiting for you at the exit from the tunnel, you could escape via the door. Clever. But like the man says it's not that clever. If Otto's waiting at the hole in the ground, he'll already have barricaded the door. And how will you know whether he's here or there? See? You'll put your mind to that later. At the moment what matters is finishing your tunnel. But Mr Otto Schnabel must not see it, otherwise he'll set a trap to catch you. So?

Your imagination is soaring, is it, dear sir? So let's have a look. Deeds follow words. Take a sufficiently wide and long plank, easily found among the panels used as try-outs for the Condottiere. Scrabble around until you find two large nails. They are found. Drive them into the masonry with the mallet you see before you, set just a little further apart than the width of the plank. Bend aforementioned nails. Slide plank between them. Push. The plank hits the soil, the nails hold it in place like pegs. Dig out the soil that's just underneath. As you dig, the plank advances. And the tunnel, thanks to man's genius, is now sheltered by just a thin layer of soil – as long as you've reckoned it right – supported by the plank. Otto sees nothing. And when you've decided it's time to emerge, you retract the plank. The soil collapses. An ocean of light floods into the room. A gaping hole appears.

An hour will go by. And in an hour's time? Mr Gaspard Winckler, you are free. A feeling he will never have known, something unlike anything else . . . He'll be lost in his freedom. He'll drown in it. He'll walk the roads. He'll be a vagrant. He'll be totally bewildered . . .

What do you look like as you do it? You raise your arm, you bring it down, you drag a small amount of soil and a bit of mud towards you, you push the plank forward an inch, you slide along, you wriggle about like an earthworm, like a snake in the grass. What do you look like, half naked, with something like a cake-slicer in your hand, making mud pies like a boy on a beach. An uncomfortable position. It's hot. You must be very dirty. What a busy day you've had! Do you remember Jérôme? Do you remember Rufus? Do you remember Madera? Do you remember Geneviève? Mila? Nicolas? Do you remember Split, Geneva, Paris? Do you remember Giottino,

Memling, Cranach, Botticelli, Antonello? Do you remember the Three Magi, the Madonnas and Child, the Christ the Kings, the Resurrections, Donors, Princes, Princesses, Fools and Retinue, the Bremen Burghers, the Knights of the Sepulchre, the *Déjeuners sur L'Herbe*, the Bridges near Blois, the Three Peaches on a Table, the Boats at Saint-Omer? Do you remember the Masonic chests, the totems, the Upper Volta wood carvings, the Jamaican Three Pence Brown, or the sesterces of Diocletian? Do you remember Gstaad and Altenberg? Do you remember your life?

His hands and his eyes. Anything by anybody from any period. All his own work. All of it, but nothing else. Gaspard the forger. Italian specialities. That dead crowd that had been robbed and betrayed. Cleaned out. Gaspard the forger. Roll up, roll up, the whole world is on show. Admire. The man who knows it all. The only person who managed to copy the Mona Lisa's smile, to unravel the secrets of the Incas, to learn the forgotten techniques of Aurignacian man. Come and see the history of art in one volume. Gaspard the forger. Gaspard Winckler. Period media and backing. Works on commission . . .

The rest would be lost in a guffaw. Forger. *Faussaire. Fausse ère*: wrong period. Bad times. Storm on the way. A forger's forger. Necrophagist . . .

Any answer? Anything certain? Anything obvious? No. Not yet. Not even an acceptable fact. Not quite a done deal. It's as if having been a prisoner for years in an underground cell far from light and life – in the cellars of Split and Sarajevo, and the studio at Dampierre – he'd been getting ready for his escape for months, years, centuries, ages, by means of a tunnel, a passage through the earth, and that the coming moment would be the drawn-out unfolding of his own body in damp clay, dirt, fatigue, discouragement, obstinacy, and cramp. Then a hoarse breathing sound. Despair. For hours and hours perhaps. Then a layer of sod collapses, the sky appears, grass, wind, night . . .

Something that will not necessarily be called freedom, just something alive, a tiny bit more alive; something that will not quite be courage, but will no longer be cowardice. Potential at a stroke, because at a stroke age-old barriers will fall. Something that would be his, and only his, that would come only from him and would be his business and nobody else's. Himself, without the others: no more Jérôme, no more Rufus, no more Madera . . .

Because failure was born one day in acute and precise self-awareness from overweening ambition, because the Condottiere turned out to be nothing more than a bounder, a disarmed horseman, a sad country squire lacking all strength, the world had suddenly lost all meaning. What had he been expecting? What had he been trying to do? Had he never been free? Had he had to go through Jérôme dying and Geneviève leaving, had he had to see the Condottiere turn into a failure and see Madera die before he noticed? Did he know that? Could he see that? What had begun? What was more important? Did his conscience remember only to protect itself . . .

One by one your memories are wasting away. What? Who started it? Who joined in the game? Who put his head in the sand so as not to see what was going on?

The failure of the Condottiere, the death of Madera. Same thing? The same outpouring of hatred and madness . . .

He has reached the end of his plank. Everything is ready. One shove, and the earth will fall in. The way will be clear . . .

But Otto will be standing there, a few centimetres or a few metres away from you, and he'll be ready to fire, not to kill you, for sure, but to stop you getting away. You wonder what to do. If Otto is somewhere near the tunnel exit, he is sure to have secured all the doors. He can't not be at the tunnel exit, since he can't not have heard you digging. If you dig a tunnel it's to get away through it, so he'll be standing guard outside it. But as he's by no means so stupid as not to imagine there might be a trap, he will have bolted the door of Madera's study, at the top of the stairs. Suppose you went up to that door, taking down the barricade you've set up to secure the lower door, and made as much noise as possible in doing so? He'll come back in. And while he's on his way back inside the house, whoosh! You go back down at top speed, pull out the plank and off you go. No? No. There's not enough time. It's not precise enough. Let's think it through again. Point one: Otto is at the tunnel exit, or rather, because he doesn't know exactly where it is he's relied on the sound and having worked out that the tunnel is being dug under this wall has taken up position a few metres away so as to be able to watch the whole length of the wall. Otto must be near the tunnel. You have to bet that Otto is near the tunnel. Point two: Otto's looking out for you. He's expecting you to emerge from the tunnel, he's shut off the other exits, and he won't budge for all the gold in Peru. Point three: you have to make him budge. It all boils down to that. You have to get Otto to budge. You've reached the age of thirty-three and the only issue on your plate – and if anything is a crucial issue, this is it – is to cause the man known as Otto Schnabel, age fifty, weight 80 kg, indeterminate nationality, formerly butler to Anatole Madera, to change his position for a few seconds, but a few minutes would be better. Yes. But how. You could call him. But he wouldn't respond. You could put a white sheet over your head and emerge and he might think it was a ghost, you'd go hoo! hoo! he'd panic and take to his heels and you'd been home and dry. But you're way off there. How? Come on. You can batter down the first door. But what if he's block-aded the garden gate? He'll hear you, he'll rush in and shoot you in the legs. He'll get you . . .

Can you feel the seconds ticking away, the minutes trickling past? Have you got your mind on it properly, Gaspard Winckler? You've got your grey matter up to speed, haven't you? Dura mater, pia mater, etcetera. Have you got the answer? You've got it. It's very simple . . .

Let's go over it again. Let's keep it short and logical. Order, precision, method. You are about to carry off your greatest coup.

What's the one thing that would make Otto shift himself? Rufus. Rufus, obviously. Rufus is not here. But Otto is expecting Rufus. Let's suppose Rufus goes back to his hotel. The concierge will certainly tell him that someone called Otto Schnabel has called several times. And left a message. Come to Dampierre fast. Obviously Otto hasn't said: Madera has just been murdered. That's not the kind of thing you say out loud. What does Rufus do? He calls Otto. What's Otto doing now? He's keeping watch on you while waiting for Rufus to call back. So? So you take the phone and set it up on the workbench. Then you get a travelling bag and stuff into it the keys to your apartment, money, your electric shaver, a shirt, tie and sweater. You place it all on the workbench. You take the bag with you; as soon as you're out you'll clean off the dust and mud that'll be more or less all over you. Do you remember the route? Is everything clear in your mind? What have you forgotten? Check. Your papers? Cigarettes? Matches? You go back down. You go back up. You take a long deep breath. Are you in a panic? You are not in a panic . . .

Wind up the phone. Dring dring dring. You have to trust that Otto is outside at the tunnel exit otherwise he will have heard the office telephone going click as you make the call . . . Good afternoon, operator, this is Dampierre 15 on the line. I don't think my phone is working properly. One of my friends insists he called me three or four times this morning – he got here by car this afternoon – but I didn't hear anything . . . Can you call me back in ten seconds' time? Ten seconds, alright. Yes, operator, Dampierre 15. Madera is the name. Thank you, operator, speak to you soon.

Ten seconds. You hang up. Your heart is beating. You look at your wristwatch. Nine. Heads or tails? Eight. What are you betting on it working? My kingdom for a. Seven. Six. If logic is in charge then it has to work. Four. But then. I killed. Three. Madera. Two. Now time speeds up. Go in a flash. Zero. It's ringing. Far far far away. He's heard it. He's running. He's sure it's Rufus. Give him time to turn the corner. One. Two three. Take away the plank. Pick up your bag. Put your head out. There you are. There you are. There you are! Run! One two three four five metres. Thank you and goodbye. Ten eleven twelve. Slide under the fence. There you are. Don't come a cropper in the grass. Run. Say hello to the Eiffel Tower for me. Don't look round don't look round don't look round.

But now everything was dropping and slipping away from him, perhaps as a rebound from a hope that had been nurtured for too long. The life that for a moment he had thought he held in his hands, that compact, dense sum of collected memories, his quest, had shattered into a million pieces, into self-directing meteorites, each with its own life from now on, maybe still connected to his own but ruled by mysterious laws whose constants he did not know. Once again memories sharpened and then suddenly exploded and split up into a myriad impressions, into fragments of life it would have been fruitless to try to make sense of, give direction to, or separate from each other. Splinters and shreds. As if the landscape of his past life had just suffered a cataclysm. As if he no longer had the world in his arms. Did not yet have the world in his arms. He had entered a new era.

This deep chaos was like the chords played by an orchestra before the conductor mounts the podium, with each instrument practising the first bars of its own part, tuning strings, reeds, valves, trying out scales, testing chords as if to underscore the inorganic caterwaul out of which, very soon, because they will all be under the direction of a conductor who will assert his presence, because they will go back to and follow the coherence of the composer's score, there will spring, in reimposed silence and with the house lights down, the living work itself, the voluntary burst of the trumpets and horns, the plenitude of the quartet and the rhythm that the timpani extract from time and turn into a tempo. If that were so, if that should turn out to be so, then, because he would finally have plumbed the lowest depth of his own madness, his acknowledgement of chaos would finally give birth to a firm grasp of himself and of the world in all its splendour and strength. Has he won? Not yet. He's free and on an empty road. He's walking on without knowing where he's going. It's dark. It's just before eight o'clock. Madera is dead. In the laboratory, in a corner, the absurd, abandoned, already dusty *Portrait of a Man* is scowling. A useless gesture or a step in the right direction? He does not know. He nods his head. He is cold . . .

You're going to walk to Châteauneuf. You'll get a taxi to take you on to Dreux. You won't catch a train. Too big a risk that you'll bump right into Otto waiting for you at the station. You'll look for a lorry driver willing to give you a lift to Paris. You'll be in Paris tonight. What then? You'll see. You don't know. Are you scared?

For years on end the dead weight of days going by. A story as old as the hills? Your arm raised . . . Day after day, and then this business, this fate, this caricature of a destiny . . . The end. Avoidable, or unavoidable? Then what? Then nothing. Not enough time to think. Not enough time even to know. You wanted to live. You are living. You wanted to leave. You got out. Madera is dead and Rufus is miles away. So what? Now you're on your own in the middle of the night.

What's the point of consciousness? Were you happy, Gaspard Winckler? Are you happy? Will you be happy? Night looks like nothing on earth. You're walking by the side of the road. You're flagging down the few cars that go past. They're not stopping. How long will you go on walking? Are you going to die in the ditch? Are you going to lie down in the middle of the road in the hope that a grey Porsche, hunting you down at 120 kilometres per hour, will run you over without even noticing? Where is Rufus? Has he got back to his hotel? Mr Rufus Koenig likes to go to bed early. But he's not going to get a lot of shut-eye tonight . . .

You're getting on my nerves, Gaspard Winckler. You weren't much good except at forgeries. Now you're free, what are you going to be able do? What kind of nonsense? It worries you. You'd like to understand. There's nothing to understand. It's too cold to think. You'll think about it tomorrow. Or never. You'll find out, one day . . .

In the half-light, to begin with, he had used each hand to put the glove on the other. He had done all he had planned . . . He had gone up the stairs, step by step. He had pushed the door open in silence. The thick carpet had muffled the noise of his feet. With his left hand he had grabbed Madera by the neck and pulled his head back while his right hand, the one that had been gripping the razor for some time already – a little too tightly – thrust it forward and in an insanely rapid slash slit the neck that presented itself to him, a thick neck with fleshy folds overhanging the white silk shirt. And blood spurted out as if from an abscess that had burst. Open anthrax. Blood streaming out, covering everything in a thick pulsing stream, coating the desk, the calendar, the white telephone, the glass panel, the carpet, the armchair. Blood, black and warm, as alive as a snake or a squid, trickling between the chair legs. And a sudden burst of joy, like a cannon shot, a joy bursting out like a drumroll, like a trumpet encore. That total, radiant, crazy feeling of joy. Incomprehensible. So comprehensible.

So comprehensible ... Isn't that right, Gaspard Winckler?

Foundering brutally at full steam, as if the whole world or, if not the world, then the moderately sickening universe of the room were plunging into the void, the laboratory, that immense and empty studio, re-emerged as another kind of prison: a microcosm featuring contradictions drawn, quartered and individually displayed on a wall, as if, *in fine*, those evil, clunky reproductions of the Condottiere on the high, sheer walls, those reduplicated images of a face of triumph and control, were, on reflection, ill-matched by the living image of failure on the unfinished panel set on its special easel with its four corners protected by a triple sheath of cotton wool, rag cloth and metal angle-piece at the carefully contrived focal point of six small spotlights: it didn't show unity restored, the mastery of the world or inalterable permanence, but instead, a mere frozen flash – as if catching sight of itself in a moment of clarity – portraying the fundamental anguish of blind force, the sourness of cruel might, and doubt. It made it seem that Antonello da Messina had wanted, in total disregard of the most obvious law of history and four hundred years before time, to express in their incomplete fullness all the anguished contradictions of consciousness. Every contradiction under the sun seemed to have settled into the mirror of the face portrayed, but they were just absurd, insignificant contradictions precisely because they were expressed through techniques that should have only ever been adequate to portray unambiguous certainties. The painting did not show a warlord looking beyond the portraitist towards the world with all the irony, cruelty and impassiveness of a mind at one with itself; it did not reveal a painter who had summoned up in palpable form and structure above and beyond his model the eternal, rational stability of a Renaissance: it was the double, triple, quadruple game of a fake artist pastiching his own pastiche, but by transcending pastiche and reaching out beyond his subject and beyond his own intellectual grasp and ambition, finding only the murky ambiguity of his own self. Impassiveness had turned into panic, the relaxed firmness of the muscles had come out as lockjaw, the look of confidence had become arrogance and the firmness of the mouth now expressed revenge. Every detail was no longer an integral element of an irreducibly transcendent totality, but just a flimsy and fleeting trace of a man's will strained to breaking point, a will that was itself rendered untrue by its development, wearing ever thinner as the superficial impression of completeness gave way to distorting elements which by virtue of their power and ambiguity undermined, point by point, the apparent harmony of the ensemble. This was not an artist grasping the world and his own self in a single glance; it was the somewhat haphazard and decidedly murky back-and-forth of a constructed ambiguity, of a hoax, of a crude piece of fakery, where the artist was just a minor demon of truth made uncertain, the clumsy demiurge of a structure so fragile that hardly had it emerged from chaos than it sank back into it with all the inhuman force of suffered defeats, half-intentional mistakes, and self-consciously broken bounds. All the meticulous hierarchy of the lighting, the admirable layout of the planes, the superb implementation of technique – the glues and plaster used for the *gesso duro*, the mixing dishes, the herbs and soils, the spatulas and brushes, the rags, preparatory drawings and trial canvases, the pencil sketches, charcoal sketches, pastel paints, caulks, oils, glazes, eyeshades, magnifying glasses, and arm-supports – were only symptoms of the project's futility. From the centre of the painted panel shone forth sacrilegious self-satisfaction. In the now empty laboratory the failure had been entire.

II

"I'm lost, Streten. I've lost the thread. It was all a terrible mess, I feel I've lost everything, as if it's all collapsed and I've got nothing left. I don't know what I was trying to do, I don't know where I am anymore. Things seemed to happen too fast, I couldn't keep up, I had no time to take a different path, it all happened outside of me – do you see?"

"What were you after? What were you looking for?"

"I don't know . . . To make a break . . . make a clean break. Smash everything. Leave nothing behind me . . ."

"That's what you did . . ."

"Perhaps . . . But I don't understand it, I don't understand now why it was the only thing I could do . . . I should have burst out laughing, don't you see, I should have felt relieved, released . . . But I didn't . . . It had no meaning; it was completely gratuitous. It didn't add up to anything. One move too many, a step too far. A feeling that I should have stopped beforehand . . . Madera's death had to have a meaning, but wanting to make it meaningful just made the muddle worse . . . I was digging a hole in the wall of the laboratory, I didn't know why; I told myself I was in mortal danger, but it wasn't true. Otto would never have killed me, and if Rufus had turned up he would surely not have turned me over to the police. So everything I was doing was absurd. Everything I'd done. Not just killing Madera, but everything I'd done for years. I didn't get it. I was in a complete panic; the only things I managed to tell myself were idiotic kinds of encouragement, or puns. Or dumb questions. I got lost in the details. I just sneered at myself and the next minute felt sorry for myself. One minute something would depress me, the next minute I thought it was all quite funny. Then I got out, started running, got to the road, and began to walk. All of a sudden on the road in the middle of the night I felt lonely. It didn't make any sense. Something I didn't feel, that I thought I would never feel. All of a sudden, utterly inexplicably, loneliness. Fear of being alone. And it went on all night, and the next day, and the days after. At home, on the train, on the boat that brought me to Split, and all the next night on the train, until I got here. Do you see? Not just any kind of loneliness. Loneliness like Jérôme's at Annemasse: complete, unremitting aloneness, because there was nothing for me to hang on to, because I had no idea how I was going to live, what I was going to do, how I would fill my days, who I would see, where I would stay. Completely at a loss. In utter disarray . . ."

"And now?"

"Nothing's changed, although I'm calmer . . . It's easier, that's all . . ."

"Are you going to stay here?"

"Maybe . . . If I can find work . . . It's not very important, for the time being I've got enough money not to need to work for a few months."

"Are you going to go back to being a forger?"

"No. Definitely not."

"Why not?"

"I don't know . . . Because everything is logical, after all . . . If I hadn't been a forger none of this would have happened . . ."

"Why not?"

"I don't know . . . It's obvious . . ."

"Obvious?"

"Yes . . . more or less obvious. Forging isn't a trade. It's more like a rut. You get stuck in it. You get drowned. You think things are still possible . . . But you get tripped up by your own rope-trick. Things don't exist anymore . . . It's difficult to explain . . . How can I say . . . You always do the same thing, you explore the same paths over and over, you hit the same blocks again and again. You think you overcome some of them, but actually each time you just dig yourself in deeper. You never get to being yourself, you're always someone else. Over and over again. For ever. With no hope of ever being anything more than a perfect duplicator. It had no purpose, it didn't lead anywhere . . ."

"It earned you a living . . ."

"Sure . . . It also provided an income for Jérôme and Rufus and Madera. But that's not a reason. It didn't mean anything . . ."

"You chose to live that way . . ."

"Yes, I did choose it . . . How could I have known? I've been a forger for twelve years. I've been piling up falsities for twelve years . . ."

"You killed Madera because you wanted to stop being a forger?"

"Why not? For that reason, and for other reasons. For that reason amongst others, will that do? I really don't know . . . I killed him, and that's all there is to it."

"That's too simple. You must have had something in your mind when you decided to kill him."

"Why should I have had anything in my mind? I wasn't thinking about anything, I was thinking about everything and nothing . . . You have to understand . . . It wasn't something normal . . . It wasn't something I wanted to do, it was a thing I was doing. I didn't think, I hadn't ever thought about it . . . I don't know how to put this . . . it was compulsory, I couldn't say no to it, I couldn't keep on saying no to it. It was a sort of final solution, do you see, the last possible act . . ."

"Why?"

"Because he was right there, because I couldn't stand him, I was completely sick of him, because I couldn't put up with anything . . . You think it's easy . . . You think it'll sort itself out . . . you think there are straightforward solutions, and happy endings . . . But there aren't . . . Nothing just comes to you . . . You do something, anything . . . not knowing why . . . But after a while the thing is behind you, it's altered you, and you have to take it into account. You have to justify it and claim it as your own. Accept it."

"What thing?"

"Whatever. The *Portrait of a Man*, for instance. Coming back from Gstaad in the middle of the night. Or Madera's death. Any one of the things I've done over the last twelve years . . . it was too easy. I had layers of protection wrapped around me. I didn't have to answer to anybody. Always incognito. Always innocent. And then it went wrong. Now I have to start again and I have to explain, I have to explain every last act, every last choice, every last decision I make. For the first time in my life I've got no protection. Don't have any more alibis. For twelve years I never asked myself any questions apart from questions about the fakes I had on my worksheet. Now I find I was guilty . . ."

"Guilty of what?"

"Of anything you like . . . Of Madera's death and my own acts . . . Guilty of having slipped behind him with a razor in my hand, of having slit his throat. Guilty of not knowing the reason why and of not wanting to know the reason why. Guilty of letting myself get dragged into this barren adventure, of not having tried to understand it sooner, of not having tried to change the course of events . . . How am I supposed to know? . . . It got to a point where everything collapsed in one go, a point where all I could see was Madera's death, because everything had come crashing down, and I had to take my revenge!"

"On him?"

"On him. I had to take it out on someone. On him, because someone had to pay. Rufus and Madera had been propping me up for years and doing nothing to let me get away, quite the opposite, they had been doing all they could to ensure I had everything I needed and felt safe. And they were living off me, off my work and my illusions. They'd played along with me for years, cultivated my penchant for living incognito, the absurd wish I had only to live behind multiple masks, to make a life out of hiding behind the remains of dead men. They'd been trying for years not to help me but to get me to sink deeper, they'd been watching me go under . . ."

"Why were you going under?"

"I was living in a false world, Streten, I was living in a world without sense. I spent my time in galleries and studios. I spent my whole time making a precise study of acts that others had performed long before, and performed better, in the vain but well-paid belief that I could match them perfectly. Listen. I did not exist. Gaspard Winckler was a name without content. No police force was out to get me, nobody even knew who I was. I had no country, no friends, no aims. Once a year I did a genuine restoration job for the Art Museum in Geneva. I was supposed to be off sick for the rest of the time. Where my money came from nobody knew. I was allegedly on Rufus's payroll as the picture restorer at his art gallery, but everyone knew that the Koenig Gallery hardly ever needed to do restoration work on its holdings. I was the world's greatest forger because nobody knew I was a forger . . . That's all. That's enough . . ."

"Enough to go under?"

"Enough to be dead. I was guaranteed to get away with it provided no-one guessed that I existed. It went on for twelve years. Why twelve, I've no idea. Why twelve years instead of a whole life, like Jérôme's, I don't know. But after twelve years I'd had my fill. I couldn't go on, you see. I could not keep going. I needed actions that were mine alone, I needed a life that belonged to me and to nobody else. But that was baloney; I'd set things up so that it could never come about, so that there was no exit. Do you see: caught in my own trap! There was no method for starting again, no way of saying no, of going back to square one."

"Why not? You could easily have refused to work for Rufus and Madera..."

"No. I couldn't refuse. I wanted to say no. At times I made up my mind to say no. But I couldn't do it."

"Why not?"

"I don't know..."

"When did you make up your mind to say no more?"

"The first time was in September two years ago, straight after leaving your studio. I remember, I was in the plane en route for Paris. I was late going back, I hadn't warned anyone, not even Geneviève, and I hadn't even answered her when she'd asked me ten days earlier to come back as quickly as I could. The plane made a stop in Geneva and I sent a telegram to Geneviève and another one to Rufus. Geneviève wasn't at the aerodrome. I went with Rufus. I should have told him that I'd just decided not to work anymore, but I didn't. There was a party at Rufus's place. He introduced me to Madera. It was the first time I'd met the man. I hadn't even known of his existence, yet I later found out that he was in fact the prime mover of the entire business and that Rufus was only the implementer and the front man. Madera proposed a deal. I didn't say anything. Rufus came over to me and asked me to accept. I nearly told him that I didn't want to, but I wanted to talk to Geneviève first. She came, I still don't know why. She didn't look at me. Nor I her. I couldn't say anything to her. She went off after a few seconds. Next day I went to see Madera. He took a little Christ by Bernadino dei Conti out of his desk and asked me to produce any Renaissance work that I liked. I said yes."

"Why?"

"I don't know. What else was I supposed to do?"

"Why did you decide to drop it?"

"To please Geneviève, I think. But it wasn't a very firm decision..."

"Did accepting Madera's deal bother you?"

"No. It didn't bother me. It didn't cheer me up either. I think at the time I couldn't care less. I think that in those days I didn't give a damn about anything..."

"Because of Geneviève?"

"Probably ... I don't know ... Probably because of her ... or because of me ..."

"Why because of you?"

"No reason ... because I took things seriously ... because of the ease with which I broke a commitment, a promise which, when I'd made it, on the plane, had seemed binding..."

"You had no respect for yourself?"

"But I did! To have lost self-respect I would have had to make a judgement about myself to begin with, and I don't think I intended or was able to do that. No, it was simpler than that, I just didn't give a damn. I stayed at home, I looked at the dei Conti, I thought vaguely about what work I would invent to stand in its stead, and that was all. I spent a week or so in that state. Now and again I leafed through Benezit's *Dictionary of Artists* searching for a painter who would fit, I made a shortlist of half a dozen, fairly obscure and uninteresting ones like d'Oggiono, Bembo, Morocini. That was when Madera phoned me and asked me first to come and work at Dampierre, and then to cook up something that could fetch a hundred and fifty million. I agreed and promised to come up with an answer a few days later ..."

"Didn't working at Dampierre bother you?"

"No. Not especially ..."

"Why did he insist on it?"

"I don't know ... I suspect he was wary of Rufus because this was a bigger deal. That must have been why he had himself introduced instead of staying in the background as he usually did."

"Had he told you at that first meeting that it would be a bigger deal than the others?"

"No, he didn't specify anything at all. He was supposed to know about the rest of the business ..."

"When he asked you for a canvas worth one hundred and fifty million, did he hint at any particular artist?"

"No. It was my choice to do an Antonello da Messina."

"Why?"

"No particular reason to start with. It was just about the only thing that could fetch the required price for that period – between 1450 and 1500 – without running the risk of making a mistake with the wood for the panel or the traces of *gesso duro* that can't be erased or with the pigments – taking into account that it had to be a painter with a high contemporary profile whose actual life was mysterious in a number of ways and whose work was easily identifiable, and so on, and finally, with a style that was accessible. It was a better choice than da Vinci, Ghirlandaio, Bellini or Veneziano. There was another advantage: there are no Antonellos in Paris, except the *Portrait of a Man known as* Le Condottiere, but there are other Antonellos all over Europe. I called Madera, who accepted an Antonello, and I asked him to fund a European tour. He said yes and I cleared off for two months."

"You wanted to clear off?"

"It made a good start. On two or three occasions I felt like sending them a telegram saying I wasn't coming back. But I didn't do it. I studied all the Antonellos diligently and then settled down in Dampierre. For a year and a half . . ."

"Why did you agree to all that so easily?"

"All what?"

"Another deal, when you'd decided to quit, settling in Dampierre when your own studio is in Geneva, and a one-hundred-and-fifty-million project when you'd chosen much less expensive guys . . ."

"I'd said yes to the new deal, so I had no reason to quibble over the rest of it. Once I've agreed to do a forgery, I don't see why I would have preferred to fake a d'Oggiono instead of an Antonello . . ."

"It takes more work . . ."

"Maybe that's what I wanted . . . Since I was saying O.K., why not go the whole hog?"

"You were going the whole hog?".

"In my own way, yes . . ."

"By deciding to do an Antonello?"

"More precisely, by deciding to do a Condottiere . . . As good a way as any of coming a cropper . . ."

"Why?"

"When I got back to Paris I decided to change the way I worked. Up till that time I'd always worked like any other forger, like van Meegeren, Icilio or Jérôme. I'd take three or four works by whomever, pick out various bits and pieces from them all, juggle them around and make a jigsaw puzzle out of them. But that didn't work for an Antonello. At the start, let's say, I had a few preconceived notions, the ones you get from a basic acquaintance with Antonello's work: his stiffness, his almost obsessive precision, the sparseness of his settings, a more Flemish than Italian distribution of mannerisms and, so to speak, an admirable command of the subject or, more exactly, a way of portraying command itself. There's nothing ambiguous or hesitant in the eyes or the gestures, only a constant assertion of poise and strength. The format of the dei Conti obliged me to do a portrait and the only one in my mind was the Condottiere. But the Condottiere is the only portrait Antonello did that is so powerful. His other portraits always fall a bit short, they're slightly more neutral, slightly more sentimental; I had no departure point for constructing my puzzle; I had just one single portrait besides which the others seemed barely more than sketches or drafts. They pointed towards the Condottiere, but that's all. I couldn't make a jigsaw . . ."

"I don't understand you . . . Couldn't you have made a puzzle-portrait out of those same drafts, as you call them, to produce something that would look like another draft of the Condottiere?"

"I wasn't interested in doing that . . ."

"Why not?"

"I don't know . . . I had this idea . . . to start from the Condottiere in order to paint another Condottiere, a different one, but of the same quality."

"That's what you called as good a way as any of coming a cropper . . ."

"Yes, of course . . . To set off on your own in search of something that only existed once and for all time . . ."

"Why did you do it?"

"Why not? I had nothing to lose. I thought I had nothing to lose . . . If I'd managed, it would have been an incredible coup."

"It was a flop?"

"It was a flop . . ."

"Why?"

"For all the reasons in the world . . . I wasn't ready . . . I wasn't good enough. Was looking for something that didn't match anything inside me, that didn't exist in me . . . What I call stiffness I can also call sincerity . . . Could I understand that face, could I understand that mastery? It didn't mean anything to me. I was just playing around, pretending to be a painter. But Antonello wasn't joking. As long as I added two and two, of course I got four . . . But I should have guessed that there was no point at all in doing sums on my own . . ."

"I don't understand you."

"Of course you don't! Nobody can understand, not even I can . . . If I'd understood, I wouldn't have tried, but if I'd understood I would have gone back as soon as Geneviève asked me to. If I'd understood I would never have followed Jérôme. If I'd understood I would have avoided Madera like the plague. If I'd understood, I would never have killed him . . . But I never understood. I had to make my own way, on my own, to the end of the road, I had to make one mistake after another, I had to pay for every action, every word, every brushstroke on every canvas, every tap of the mallet on the Hoard of Split . . . Up to the last I fought my own shadow, up to the last I tried to believe I was on the right road, I accumulated arguments, experiments, escapes and returns. I went back on my tracks. I carried on painting even when it had lost all meaning . . . I knew, but I carried on regardless. It was going wrong, but I told myself I would find out how to put it right. But what if there was no way to put it right? It was rotten to the core; if I shored things up on one side, I hit the rocks on the other, I was hitting the rocks again and again, and again, and again . . . Then one day it was all over, there was nothing that could be done about it, the house had gone up in flames and me too. There was nothing left, not a scrap to salvage. I tried to understand, I tried to understand everything, down to my most trivial actions. But the tally was easy. Zero plus zero. That's all. Twelve years of nothing. Twelve years of living as a zombie, living as Fantômas. *Nihil ex nihilo* – except that, at the end of the road, instead of a Renaissance masterpiece, instead of the portrait I thought I could perfect after twelve years' striving, instead of the only portrait I ever really wanted to paint – an image of serenity, strength, poise and command – there was a clown in a mask, a buffoon in his prime, a tense, nervous, lost, defeated, yes, utterly defeated man. That's all. It's enough. I felt as if someone had given me a gigantic slap in the face. So I responded. "

Under the spotlights the Condottiere rose from his ashes: a face decomposed and disfigured, a man demolished, an absurd lunatic who had long ceased to be a conqueror. The clear gaze and luminous scar had given way to the harsh anxiety of illegitimate leadership. No longer a man. A tyrant.

What were you after? What did you want? To extract your own image from past ages? On the back of twelve years' cumulative experience in painterly technique you wanted to pull off the authentic creation of a masterpiece? Didn't you know it was impossible, that it was a meaningless aspiration? So what. You clung on to that paltry ambition. To be at long last, in your own right, the captain of your soul and the world in an irrefutable ascent, a single movement towards unity. Just as in the past Holbein and Memling, Cranach and Chardin, Antonello and Leonardo had each launched out on his own different but identical experiment, using the same procedures and, by transcending their own creation, had managed to restore coherence and necessity. What next? Bemused by the glance that was not yours and never could be . . . To paint a Condottiere you have to be able to look where he is looking . . . You were trying to find that sense of direct conquest, the distinguishing marks of omnipotence, the look of triumph. You were trying to find that rapier-sharp look and disregarded the fact that someone had found it before you, had given an account of it, had explained it by going beyond it, had gone beyond it by explaining it. In one and the same sweep. A triumph of painting, or the painting of triumph? You were taken in by that ox-like mug, that admirably oafish face, that spectacularly thuggish snout. But what you had to recover was the strong and simple relationship (a peculiarly simplified relationship, moreover) that this personage – who was in the last analysis little more than a tarted-up barbarian – was able to afford to have with the world. Were you able to understand it? Were you able to understand why or how it occurred to this mere soldier of fortune to have his portrait painted by one of the greatest artists of his day? Could you grant that in place of unbuttoned gaudiness (with loosened doublet and aiguillettes fixed on any old how) he wore only an admirably neutral tunic with no decoration apart from a barely visible mother-of-pearl button? Could you understand the absence of a necklace, medals, or fur, the barely visible collar, the lack of pleats in the tunic, the exceptional strictness of the skull-cap? Did you grasp that the almost impossible sobriety and severity of dress had the direct consequence of leaving the face alone to define the Condottiere? Because that's what it was about. The eyes, the mouth, the tiny scar, the tensing of the muscles in the jaw were the exclusive means of giving consummate and utterly unambiguous expression to the social status, history, principles and methods of your character . . .

You had no way out. You were up against this luminous, bright face, up against just this face and no other. You, the world's greatest forger, had to reinvent it. Without cheating, without any tricks. You had to achieve the same sparseness in the clothing, the same clarity in the face. You might well have been scared. It would be no problem to get the balance and the internal logic of your painting right. No technical problems either, not even the supremely bothersome business of *gesso duro*. But the glance, the lips, the muscles? The complexion? The serenity? The look of quiet triumph and unthreatening power? The sense of presence? You had to invent. But what did you have to invent with?

Was the whole world looking at your striving? To make it work. Make what work? The unavoidable flow of time. The leap nobody had ever dared make, the step nobody had ever dared take. A monumental ambition. A monumental mistake. A vast recycling scheme. Trying to gather the central elements of your life in that face. Harmonious conclusion. Necessary conclusion. The universe of potential broached at last, beyond masks, beyond play-acting. The ambition of seeing his face emerge slowly from the wood panel, with its strength, power, and certainty. His part. You wanted to engage in combat unmasked? But you were playing a hand you'd already fixed, didn't you know that? You were trying to win but not prepared to fight . . . And who did you think you were, to go after such a win?

You accumulated reproductions, enlargements, X-rays. The Antwerp Crucifixion, the Saint Jerome from the National Gallery, the Head of a Man from Vienna, the Head of a Man from Genoa, the Munich Virgin Annunciate, the Florence portrait known as The

Humanist or The Poet, the Berlin Portrait of a Man, the Old Man from Milan, the Portrait of Man (the one with the red cap) in the Baring Collection at the National. They went round and round in your head, they weighed on your sleep, they went with you wherever you went. But at the end of the road you found nothing . . . Could you resuscitate a ghost?

You didn't know, you still don't know. You tried to cling on to your technical knowledge, but something – in you, in front of you or behind you – stopped you in your tracks. You were on your own in the studio at Dampierre. There was no Van Eyck to point the way forward . . .

"Why did you become a forger?"

"It just happened . . . I was seventeen. It was wartime. I was in Switzerland. On holiday. I'd just left the boarding school where I'd spent most of my school years and was wandering around. I met Jérôme in Berne; we became chums, more or less. He was a painter, at least that's what I thought. I was vaguely intending to enrol at the École des Beaux-Arts in Geneva. We spent a few days together; I was alone and I was bored; he had a car and took me on loads of trips. We talked art; he knew heaps of things and I knew nothing at all . . . that's what swung it . . . After a week or so he offered to train me and I said yes."

"Why?"

"I found it interesting . . ."

"What did you find interesting?"

"Anything I could learn . . . I was guaranteed better training than I would have got in any school or college."

"Did Jérôme tell you he forged paintings?"

"Yes."

"Did it bother you?"

"No . . . Why should it have bothered me? I think it amused me, more likely. "

"Why did it amuse you?"

"The allure of mystery, that sort of thing . . ."

"Do you still find it alluring?"

"Of course not, not now . . . But at the age of seventeen, why not? As good a way as any of solving problems . . ."

"What problems?"

"Oh, any old problem . . . Like going back home, that kind of thing . . . Getting set up in life . . ."

"Are you Swiss?"

"No . . . my parents sent me to Switzerland in 1939 because of the war. They'd fixed it with a banker friend of theirs in Zurich. He paid for my boarding fees and gave me my pocket money . . ."

"What did your parents do?"

"They were in business, I suppose . . . I lost interest in them a long while ago . . ."

"Why?"

"No reason . . . Oh, they were very nice . . . sent me a letter every now and then . . . for three or four years . . . They were stuck in France but then they managed to bugger off to Bermuda and the United States . . . In 1945 they had a search made to find me . . . I saw them when they changed trains . . . I was living in Geneva at that time . . . I refused to go with them and they didn't make a fuss. That's about it."

"Are they still alive?"

"I suppose so. They were in good health and there's no reason to suppose that's changed . . ."

"Do they live in Paris?"

"Presumably . . . but actually I've no idea. I haven't written to them for fourteen years . . ."

"In 1945 you were still under age . . ."

"Yes . . . but we made a private arrangement. We had no obligations to each other . . ."

"Why didn't you try to see them instead of coming here?"

"Am I a nuisance?"

"That's not why I asked the question."

"Of course not . . . Why should I have gone to see them?. . . I had no reason at all to do that . . . Can you see me getting there and saying, I've just killed a man, let me stay!"

"What would they have done?"

"I don't know and I don't care to know . . . it's of no importance whatsoever . . ."

"Perhaps . . . What happened after you agreed to work with Jérôme?"

"We went back to Geneva . . . I worked for him for two years. I helped him prepare the canvases; I learned various things: art history, aesthetics, painting techniques, sculpture, engraving, lithography. About fifteen hours a day, every day . . ."

"You liked it that much?"

"I suppose so . . ."

"What did you like?"

"Everything I was doing . . . Why, I can't say . . . Doesn't matter . . . If I hadn't liked it I suppose I would have dropped it, but it was all presented in a way that made it interesting to me . . ."

"And then?"

"At the end of two years, I left to go to the Metropolitan in New York. I stayed a year. Came back with a diploma in Painting Conservation from New York University. I did a dissertation on something or other, a dummy thesis so as to get admitted to the École du Louvre. Spent more than six months at the Louvre, so as to get a qualification, and went back to Geneva. Thanks to Rufus, and it was Jérôme who introduced us, I was appointed assistant conservation expert at the Musée des Beaux-Arts in Geneva. I stayed three months and then resigned for health reasons. All the travelling and the time spent abroad were designed to provide me with alibis. I got appointed as painting restorer at Rufus's gallery and started painting fakes. So there you are."

"You could do that all by yourself?"

"I was good enough to be Jérôme's back-up and to start working on my own. I'd had four years of apprenticeship, which is quite a lot. Over the following five years I made small things. The large-scale stuff only started later . . ."

"And what was Madera doing in the meantime?"

"Out of sight . . . According to Rufus, who told me the whole story a year ago, because I'd guessed most of it by myself, it was Madera who'd authorised Jérôme to find a number two and who'd designed the basic scenario: official apprenticeships, appointments, and so on."

"Why had he done that?"

"Apparently he had the war on his mind, and around 1943 he

could see the end coming and reckoned that the market would rise, creating more demand for paintings and more outlets for him . . ."

"Didn't Rufus or Jérôme ever say anything about this to you?"

"No. He kept completely in the background, like Nicolas, Dawnson and Speranza . . . I knew Jérôme and I knew Rufus. I knew zilch about the rest."

"Didn't you know what happened to the fakes you made?"

"I supplied them to Rufus . . ."

"You never got into trouble?"

"With the police? No . . . In Geneva Monsieur Koenig is a very respectable gentleman. His gallery is one of the most highly regarded in Europe . . ."

"Why was he a forger?"

"I've no idea . . . I never understood him . . . He didn't need the money, nor did Madera . . . Rufus made a huge pile from his gallery and Madera was supposed to be very rich anyway . . . Even if they'd made all their money from fakes, they certainly didn't need to sell any more when I started working for them . . ."

"Was the stuff you made worth a lot of money?"

"No, not much, at the beginning . . . Then it started getting more expensive . . ."

"Don't you know who bought it?"

"No . . . Private buyers, I guess. In South America, Australia . . ."

"How did it work?"

"I don't have a clue . . . Rufus ordered something from me and I provided him with what he required; for a while I would see the canvas in the art gallery storeroom and then one day it was gone and I never heard another word about it . . ."

"How were you paid?"

"I had a basic salary as a paintings restorer. To declare for taxes. Plus a percentage on the sales of the fakes I made."

"Did they all sell?"

"I suppose so. I always got . . . Between five and a hundred thousand Swiss francs per painting . . ."

"What kind of a cut was that? Twenty-five per cent?"

"Roughly . . . Five thousand for a small Degas and a hundred thousand for a Cézanne . . ."

"What did you do with all that money?"

"Nothing . . ."

"Are you hanging on to it for your old age?"

"I used to buy books . . . Books were the only things I bought very often . . . I also rented an apartment in Paris and another one in Geneva . . . I travelled a bit . . ."

"Sounds like a pretty nice life."

"Not unpleasant . . ."

"What was wrong with it?"

"There was nothing wrong with it . . . I think that was the worst thing about it . . . Everything was completely fine, it went like clockwork. An interesting job, good money, long holidays, foreign travel . . ."

"But there must have been something wrong."

"Why so? Jérôme had lived his whole life like that . . . For twelve years nothing went wrong . . . It was admirably straightforward. I worked, they paid me; then I took a rest. Three weeks in some luxury hotel or a Mediterranean cruise on a yacht that Rufus would lend me. I came back, started over, and so on . . ."

"Something didn't work, all the same . . ."

"Yes, of course . . . nothing worked in the end . . ."

"But there must have been something that set it off in the wrong direction?"

"It's hard to prove . . . I've often wondered what triggered it . . . But that doesn't make a lot of sense . . ."

"Why not?"

"I don't know . . . It would take too long to explain . . . I'd have to remember what I was thinking on a given day, at a given time . . . but I don't remember . . ."

"What day, what time?"

"Any day . . . Any time . . . Any year . . . While I was at work or when I was off . . . What I was thinking, what I wanted to do, what I wanted to achieve . . . It's really too hard . . . At the start it all went smoothly . . . But it wasn't right . . . I don't know why, I don't even know what that means . . . It wasn't right, there was something missing, something I wanted but couldn't or could no longer have . . . I can't find my words . . . a kind of . . . a kind of agreement with myself, a kind of peace . . . a match . . . some such thing . . . It's not that I ever felt guilt . . . no, that's not it, not at all . . . making fakes never weighed on my conscience . . . I'd rather make fake Chardins than authentic Vieira da Silvas any day . . . If I'd been a real artist I doubt I would ever have done anything that would have made a mark ... I'd been convinced of that for years ... but that's not what the issue was ... What I did was meaningless, but that's not what mattered ... It's not easy to put this into words ... What I was doing wasn't going anywhere ... I had no chance of getting out of it ... All I could do was to go right the way through Benezit's *Dictionary*. Every painter, every engraver, every sculptor. In alphabetical order ... do you see? Antonello, Bellini, Corot, Degas, Ernst, Flémalle, Goya ... etcetera, you see ... Like kids who play at finding a writer, a painter, a musician, a capital, a river and a country that all begin with the same letter ... So there you are. I was condemned to carrying on an idiotic game ..."

"It made you a very nice living."

"So what? It made me a living, alas ... If I'd been starving, then of course I wouldn't have gone on with it ... But I was snug as a bug in a rug ... So obvious ... The goose that laid the golden eggs, updated ... They'd got the hang of it ..."

"Why do you pretend to be a victim?"

"Why shouldn't I? I fell for it at the age of seventeen and that was that. That Madera was too polite to be honest ... Come this way, my lad, if you'd like to be a painter ..."

"That works on a seventeen-year-old ... But when you were twenty? Twenty-three? Thirty?"

"That's what I told myself too ... But what could I do about it? Once you're in a rut ..."

"That doesn't mean anything. Are you trying to tell me that you didn't at any point have the strength to say no?"

"Why say no? The strength to say no to what? What good would it have done me? What would I have lived on . . . ? You don't understand . . . I did say no . . . a week ago . . . I killed Madera because I was saying no . . . I killed Madera because there was no other way I could say no . . ."

"That's too easy . . ."

"Too easy? You can talk! Too easy to let everything fall to pieces! Too easy to feel you're going bonkers? I didn't do anything, Streten, I didn't do anything because there was nothing I could do . . . Believe me, I was strapped in place. Strapped tight. No room to move. Not to the left, not to the right. I couldn't move a finger on my own . . ."

"That's not what I meant, Gaspard, as you know very well . . . It's too easy to say, after having killed Madera, that there was nothing else you could do. You didn't try to do anything else . . ."

"How do you know? I tried to say no but I couldn't . . ."

"Why not?"

"Because it was meaningless . . ."

"Did killing Madera have a meaning, then?"

"Did accepting Jérôme's offer have a meaning? Things happened the way they happened. That's all. I met Jérôme and I agreed to work with him. It was a trap. Twelve years later I realised it was a trap. I couldn't unspring it. That's all . . ."

"That's still too simple. How did you come to realise it was a trap?"

"Like any man in the world, I suppose, I sought happiness. Like any man I also wanted a suitable position in life. I got a position that suited me. But I was not happy . . ."

"Why weren't you happy? How did your not being happy manifest itself from day to day?"

"I haven't the faintest idea."

"You're lying . . . That doesn't mean anything . . . You're not telling your story properly . . . You're overdoing it . . . For sixteen years, four in apprenticeship, twelve in the trade, you lived in a world of your own choosing . . . After sixteen years you say that the whole enterprise hit the rocks . . . But that can't be true . . . There was something that set it off, something that started the ball rolling. It's all very well to let yourself be caught in a trap, but there was no reason you should have noticed. It doesn't make sense. If it had all been natural you'd have carried on as a forger for the rest of your life, like Jérôme . . . Do you see what I mean?"

"Of course . . . You'd like there to be a solid point of departure, a sudden insight . . . But that's not right either . . . As the days went by, nothing happened . . . There wasn't any turning point in my existence . . . There wasn't a story . . . There wasn't even an existence . . . Of course, if things had been logical, I would never have been able to acknowledge my own weakness, I would never have felt the ground give way under my feet, I'd never have been aware of anything at all . . . It's just that I wanted to live. In spite of them, in spite of Rufus, in spite of Madera, I wanted to be something more than a duplicator, a plagiarist, the man with the magic hands . . . To be something other than anything by anybody from any period . . ."

"What did you mean when you said 'I wanted to live'?"

"Nothing at all, and that's the point ... that is the question. That's it in a nutshell ... 'being alive' is meaningless when you're a forger. It means living with the dead, it means being dead, it means knowing the dead, it means being anyone at all. Vermeer or Chardin. It means spending a day or a month or a year inside the skin of an Italian from the Renaissance, or a Third Republic Frenchman, or a German from the Reformation, or a Spaniard or a Dutchman. It means inserting a few additional details into that man's life, a more or less coherent set of facts, something plausible in between two more definite facts: where was Memling before he got to Bruges? On the Rhine? Did he paint when he was there? Of course he did. Why shouldn't he have produced a Virgin with a Donor in Cologne around 1477? You do research and find that in the present state of knowledge, it could fit; so you take off for Bruges to spend three weeks at the Sintjanshospitaal studying the Virgin with Apple and the Shrine of St Ursula and so on; you come back, and six months later in the attic of a more or less deserted convent near Cologne someone discovers a Virgin that looks quite like Marie Morel and Donor with looks somewhere between those of that thug in the Rijksmuseum and Martin Van Der Whatsit, the Burgomaster of Bruges and a Donor himself. That's how it's done, and it doesn't mean a thing ... But day and night for six whole months, awake and asleep, you've been Hans Memling, or Memlinc if you insist. You've put yourself in his shoes and travelled the same path in reverse ... Gaspard Winckler, who's he? ... It was like that all through those twelve years ... It wasn't painful, it wasn't dreadful, it was fascinating, stimulating, tremendous ... But I couldn't carry on with it ... You must understand, I spent my time making impressions ... I just took a blank patch, a missing beat, a hole in some other painter's life with a rather vague date and slightly elastic data, and there you go, I would slip into his tunic ... It was all useless, the precautions were pointless because three out of four buyers took Rufus or Madera or their front men at their word. They could have checked if they'd wanted to and it would have worked. We knew the rules of the game inside out. We didn't take any risks, we had accounts and files. We knew where to check if the need arose. As a picture restorer I was entitled to go into archives and to search in museum storerooms. But at the end of the day I was still underwater ... I was the sum total of all the dubious parts ... Even more than the fourteenth guest ... I turned up just in time to paper over the gaps ... But my own life ... I was ambitious ... not even ... even if I took every precaution, I was Gaspard Winckler nonetheless ... I needed something else ... You can't hold it against me ..."

"Needed what?"

"To be me ..."

"What did you need so as to be you?"

"I don't know ... That's why it was a trap ... The self was left out of it, it didn't count. I was just a hand, a performing tool. What I brought were my dictionaries, file cards, brushes and paint pots. But in real life I wanted some fine day or night to be able to rip off my mask and be something other than a forger ... It stuck to my skin, everywhere I went it followed behind . . . Who are you? I am nobody, I am anybody . . ."

"It's what you wanted . . ."

"Yes, I'd wanted it, really wanted it . . . I'd wanted to erase myself, make myself disappear . . . I'd wanted to be everybody so as to end up as nobody, I'd wanted to protect myself beneath innumerable masks, to be inaccessible, to be impregnable . . . The result? I went too far . . . It was asking too much to get away with it entirely, there were bound to be domains where it didn't work . . ."

"Which domains?"

"I met Mila, I never should have . . . She didn't pick me up: I was the one who went after her. That was my first mistake . . . Being a forger means taking everything from other people and giving nothing of yourself . . . I gave Mila nothing . . . I didn't pay attention, I remained indifferent. It was natural. I went after her. She came to me. I plodded on down my own path. Why should I have swerved to the left or right? She left. I missed her. So what? At the time I was working on the Hoard of Split. I was very busy. That's all."

"Was it serious?"

"No. Why should it be serious? It was almost natural . . . a tiny slip of the steering . . . Did I love Mila? I've no idea, I never asked myself. I loved paintings and art books. I loved spending days and days making a fake Baldovinetti. That's what I loved . . . Didn't mean a thing. But I didn't know it was meaningless. That's how it was . . ."

"Then what?"

"Then nothing . . . Life went on as if nothing had happened . . .

Only a tiny crack had appeared in the magnificent ivory tower that protected me ... One evening I wanted to see Mila ... and I didn't dare go ... She'd left me two weeks before, without saying anything to me, for no obvious reason, simply because she expected something from me that I hadn't managed to give her ... maybe just being there ... I didn't dare and that bothered me ... I went out and spent the evening at the cinema ... That's not something I did very often ... It bored me ... I left halfway through the film, and found a bar. I had a drink. I probably had too much ... I went for a walk along the street ... At Place de la Madeleine I picked up a girl and took her home. In the morning I told myself I'd been an idiot and ought to have stayed at home and got on with some work. Which is what I did on the evenings that followed."

"Was the work going well?"

"Extremely well ... You're amazed, aren't you? You think it would make better sense if I'd been working poorly, making silly mistakes, wasting my time, or not wanting to work, or working without my heart in it ... But it wasn't so ... My ivory tower was still standing ... I was working only too well, right through the night ... That's what made sense ... plugging without delay the little wobble I'd felt ... Getting back on my usual track ... The straight track ..."

"Is that what set it all off?"

"Was that it, or was it something else? That was it, and there was also something else. It was that among other things. Tonight that was how it started because I'm telling you about it ... Something has to be the start of it . . . Why not Mila? But it could just as easily have been Jérôme getting old . . . or my slow realisation of what my true position was, the feeling that I was being used, being taken advantage of, or the simple, extremely simple accumulation of pastiches . . . masks, more masks, the burden of masks . . . The things that were stifling me without my knowing why, without my knowing what was stifling me, without my knowing that what was making me a living was the same as what was making me die . . . It's what I'd sought . . . So what? I'd sought immediate life, instant victory . . . I had to live and fight . . . I didn't want to fight . . . I was fighting in the shadows, under impenetrable armour, I was fighting against shadows. I pitted my patience against their genius. Of course I won every time. I was cheating. I didn't know I was cheating . . . But I had to wake up one day . . . It didn't matter when or where . . . It happened, it had to. It happened because of Mila, but it could have happened because of something else. It doesn't matter. It began . . . The rest is like unravelling a piece of knitwear . . . The tower collapsed, to begin with only a tiny piece broke away, but then it crumbled faster and faster . . . I tried to shore things up, to take cover, to rebuild . . . but it was pointless . . ."

I went back to France at the end of November; I spent a few days in Paris buying materials and went to Dampierre. Madera had done things properly: he had a whole section of his basement remodelled as a studio. There was a large armchair in the middle of the room with low tables on either side of it, a wonderful wood-and-steel easel, and countless spotlights. He'd had carpet laid, and put in a shower and even a telephone so I wouldn't need to be disturbed during the day. There were tables for paint pots, bookcases in every corner, more tables, a turntable, a refrigerator, another armchair, a sofa, a bed . . . It was the fairest prison you could imagine. I lived there for fifteen months and never went outside, except for a few lightning trips to Paris and Geneva. I did nothing apart from the Condottiere . . .

The start was very easy. I took ten days just to set things up: sorting out my filing cards, pinning up the reproductions I had got hold of, laying out the brushes I would use, finding the right places for paints and liquids. It all went swimmingly; I think I was more happy than not, as I always am at the start of a new job . . . Then I started to smooth down the wooden panel; that was a routine job, a tiresome one because you have to be very patient and take a lot of care. It took me ten or twelve days because I went at it very very slowly. But the panel came out almost completely blank. It was a fine piece of oak with almost no damage, so I could start on the *gesso duro* almost straight away. That was the first difficult operation. Again it was a game of patience, a steady addition of layers of plaster and glue. At the beginning of January everything was ready and I could get started on the real job; I began on plain sheets of paper, then on cardboard, trial canvases, and roughly prepared panels. I would spend part of each day copying details from the Condottiere or other Antonello portraits, and the rest of the time inventing details of my own. That's pretty much all I did for six months, without painting a single stroke. Every week I sanded the panel down a tiny bit and added a few layers of *gesso duro* to keep it in perfect readiness ... That's when it got really difficult ... I had my panel in front of me. But I was not like any other painter, and it was not like any other canvas. It was not the same as painting a windmill or a suburban landscape or a sunset ... I had to give an account of something that already existed, I had to create a new language, but I was not free: the grammar and the syntax were given, but the words had no meaning; I did not have the right to use them. That was what I had to invent, a new vocabulary, a new set of signs ... It had to be identifiable at first glance, but nonetheless it had to be different ... It was a tough game to play ...

At the start you think, or you pretend to think, it is easy. Who is Antonello da Messina? Started out in the Sicilian School, strongly influenced by Flemish painters, with secondary but still perceptible influence of the Venetian School. You can find that in any course book. It will do for a first approach. But what next? Spareness and control. That's what you tell yourself, and you think you've said it all.

But what are the signs of that sparseness? The signs of control? They don't come all by themselves. They come painfully, slowly, confusedly . . . You sit in front of your canvas or your board for hours and hours. There's nothing there except the set of laws that constrain you and that you're not allowed to break. First you have to understand them, completely, from top to bottom. Without the slightest error. You timidly venture to make a sketch. You subject it to criticism. Something's not right. You think you're changing a detail but you've made the whole structure collapse in one go. For six months I played cat and mouse with my *Portrait of a Man*. I gave him a beard, a moustache, a scar, freckles, a snub nose, a Roman nose, a flat nose, a hook nose, a Greek nose, armour, a brooch, short hair, long hair, a bonnet, a fur hat, a helmet, a drooping lip, a hare-lip . . . I could never get it right. I would look at the Condottiere. I would tell myself: look, that tautening of the muscle is such and such a shadow underscored in such and such a way with an arc of shading on the cheek, and that shading, conversely, is the whole expression of the face, its bodying forth, it's what makes one thing invisible and another thing shine out. It's from the overall play of shade and light that the facial sinews spring, packed with energy, with their own will. That was what I had to get hold of, without a model to copy. That was what struck me the most. For instance, I compared the Paris *Portrait of a Man* to the one in Vienna. It was the complete opposite. The Condottiere is a man in middle age – or rather younger, between thirty and thirty-five; whereas the Vienna portrait is of someone who is at most twenty. One is decisive, the other floppy – soft face, sunken features, receding chin, small eyes, huge bare cheeks, no muscles, no vigour. On the other hand the tunic is brighter and sharper than the face, with pleats visible as well as a brooch. I could have been wrong about the comparison, but what seemed most obvious to me was the displacement of the signs. The Vienna portrait wasn't hard to do; it could have been anyone. But the Condottiere, since it was him I'd decided to paint, had to be a face. I went round and round this realisation, I could not square the circle. To begin with I was quite taken with the idea of adorning my Condottiere with a breastplate. It would simplify a lot of things; it would allow me to play with the lighting, the grey of the breastplate and the grey of the eyes, just as in the other painting everything revolves around ochre: the headgear and the tunic, the eyes, the hair, the greenish brown background and the light ochre of the skin. I would have done a Condottiere in grey: helmet and breastplate, eyes, fairly fair hair, and very dull skin in light grey like the young man in the Botticelli at the Louvre. Only it didn't make any sense. What use did a Condottiere have for a breastplate, seeing that he was obviously sheer strength in his own right? A breastplate or cuirass was a sign, a too facile sign, just as it would have been too facile to paint him in accordance with the idea that the Romantics gave us of Italian mercenaries of the Renaissance – as a crass and boozy swashbuckling musketeer. I dropped the breastplate. I dressed him in a vaguely red tunic; but it was too close to the real one . . . I tried again . . . Every day, ten hours a day, for six months. Then I thought I'd got it. My Condottiere would be seen three-quarters, like the real one and the Vienna portrait and the Florence Humanist, hatless, the ground would be slightly more visible, the tunic would be laced but without the laces standing out, and would have a few just visible pleats at shoulder height. I settled on this costume after a great number of trials and not before going to the National Library to check whether it was actually possible. It could just about work; I could lift all the details from different works – the collar from the Vienna portrait, the tunic lacing from a Holbein, and the general configuration of the head from a Memling. The Condottiere's complexion alone took me two weeks; I couldn't pin it down; it had to match the colour of the tunic, it was supposed to set the key for all the other colours; I ended up picking a rather dull ochre, with a swarthy skin, black hair, very dark brown eyes, thick lips that were a shade darker, a *lie-de-vin* tunic, a dark red background, slightly lighter on the right hand side. Each choice entailed full-scale sketches, hesitating, pausing, backtracking, and making heroic decisions. I think I was trying to be too careful. It was all done. Ahead. With such precision that I couldn't go wrong, that the slightest touch of my brush on the wood panel would be definitive and final. That was the way I had to work, of course, but in this instance the margin for error had been completely eliminated. Any hesitation would have obliged me to start again from scratch, to sand the board down and redo the *gesso duro*. I was scared. There was something very odd about it. I'd never been scared of getting a fake wrong. On the contrary, I'd always been confident of getting it right with ease. But in this case I took whole days making up my mind about a colour, a gesture, a shadow.

The hardest part obviously was that celebrated tautness in the jaw. It was impossible to pastiche without creating a double, and there was no sense in that. In the end I settled for using Memling's portrait as my model: a very thick and powerful neck, with the first minute signs of a double chin, very deep eyes, a line on each side of the nose and a fairly thick mouth. I would put the strength into the neck, into the articulation of the head, in the very high and straight way it was held, and in the lips. It was all fine on the drafts. On the trial paintings in gouache it even turned out rather splendidly: a complex melange of Memling and Antonello sufficiently corrected, with a very pure look in the eyes, immediate contours that yielded easily at first and then thickened, became impermeable, turning hard and merciless. No cruelty, no weakness. What I wanted. Pretty much exactly what I was after . . .

It was another month before I started really painting. I had to get my pots, brushes and rags ready. I took three days' rest. I began to paint sitting in the armchair, with my palette within easy reach, and the panel set on the easel with its four corners wrapped in cotton wool and rags so that the metal angles that held it in place would leave no mark. I had an elbow support and a crutch to keep my hand steady, a huge visor to keep the glare of the spotlights off my eyes, and wore magnifying goggles. An extraordinary set of safety devices. I would paint for twenty minutes and then stop for two hours. I sweated so much I had to change three or four times a day. From then on fear never left me. I don't know why but I had no confidence at all, I never managed to have a clear vision of what I was trying to do, I couldn't say what my panel would be like when I'd finished painting it; I wasn't able to guarantee that it would look like any of the dozens of more or less completed drafts lying around the room. I didn't understand some of my own details, I was unable to get a grip on the overall project, to recognise it in the smallest touch, to feel it taking shape. I was stumbling onwards, despite the innumerable safeguards I'd set up. Previously, I'd been able to paint any Renaissance picture in a couple of months, but now, after four months' work, in mid-September, I still had the whole face to do . . .

I took eight days off; I spent five in the laboratory and three in Paris, at the Louvre and in the Archives, for no precise reason; checking details, reassuring myself about the accuracy of my collar and tunic, looking at countless books for hours on end in the search for pointless confirmation. I went back. I worked on for another two months. At the time of Jérôme's death I allowed myself another week's break; I went to London and Antwerp. Then straight to Geneva, because of Jérôme. I came back. I still had the eyes, the mouth and the neck. And the pleats in the tunic around the shoulder. I took a whole month to get them done, I'd never painted so slowly in my life. I spent hours looking at the panel. It was already a month overdue. Madera would come down more and more frequently, hovering over me, saying nothing, then he'd go out, slamming the door behind him, angry at having come upon me sitting still in my armchair with the elbow support untied and a brush hanging idly in my hand, staring for hours on end at a detail and going over in my mind the hundred or so possible strokes it would take, trying to extract a finished image from a still shapeless painted panel. Hour after hour after hour, from sunrise to nightfall, I would forget to eat, forget to drink, forget to smoke, so fascinated was I by a possible shading, obsessed by a line that was too precise, haunted by almost invisible speckling . . . At the end of the year I took another two days' off. On January 1, I began the mouth. On February 1, I started on the shading of the neck. I think I was too tired and too nervous and too edgy to do anything worthwhile. On February 20, I stopped almost completely. I looked at the Condottiere for five days running. He was still missing his eyes and all the muscle-lines in his neck . . . It was possible he could be completed . . . It was still possible he would be completed . . . I pushed away the armchair, the side-tables and the elbow-crutch. The easel stood on its own in the middle of the room. Like a gallows. In the morning of February 25, I started painting standing up, without a visor and without a magnifying eye-piece, with a dozen different brushes and a palette. Within the day, almost without a break, I finished the neck and the eyes. By the evening it was almost entirely done, there were just some tiny details left. After that I would just have to put on the glaze and then bake it to make the craquelure appear. I thought I had carried it off. I wasn't particularly proud. I wasn't particularly happy. I was exhausted, shattered. Buggered. Something I couldn't resist, the feeling that it wasn't right, that I'd lost the thread, that the Condottiere wasn't what he should have been. As if I'd made a complete mess that I hadn't been able to see, and it was too late now. I went to bed. I woke up in the middle of the night. I switched on a single spotlight. I looked at my Condottiere . . .

"And then?"

"Then nothing . . . It wasn't right . . . Not right at all . . ."

"Why?"

"I don't know . . . it was the converse, or the inverse . . . just a guy with a pale face, a miserable chap . . ."

"You'd never noticed before?"

"No . . . I'd never seen him before . . . A rat . . . A rat with resentful eyes . . . it was anything . . . anyone . . . a convict released after fifteen years inside . . ."

"But didn't you believe just a few hours before that you'd succeeded?"

"A few hours before, yes I did . . . But that didn't mean anything! It was a high! I'd done my homework . . . it was the satisfaction at having got it off my back . . ."

"Did Madera see the Condottiere?"

"Yes . . . the next morning."

"What did he say to you about it?"

"Nothing . . . He said nothing . . . I was lying on the bed fully dressed, with my tie nearly strangling me, dead drunk, surrounded by empty bottles, stubbed cigarettes and puke . . . I was dead drunk . . . He called Otto who made me take a dozen showers and down a litre of coffee . . ."

"Why did you get drunk?"

"To celebrate my great victory ... To celebrate my admirable triumph ... The sensational end-piece of twelve years' sterling service ..."

"Why did you get drunk?"

"What else did I have to do? I'd been sleeping next to those awful guys for eighteen months ... For eighteen months I'd been frantically trying to get the last one of all ... It hadn't worked, it was a complete mess ... What else would you have had me do? You think I should have slept like a log? And had a lovely dream? I was finished. Washed up. Done for. Done in. Down and out."

"How do you know the Condottiere was a mess?"

"I saw it ..."

"You saw it twice ... The first time you thought it was a success, then you wake up in the middle of the night and realise it's a failure ..."

"If it had been right why would I not have seen that twice in a row?"

"Because you wanted it to be a failure ..."

"That's too easy, Streten ... I can see what you're getting at ... But I'd spent eighteen months struggling with it ..."

"What does that prove?"

"It proves I wanted to get it right ... Hindsight makes it tempting to say I must have done it on purpose ... But all I put into it was only done because I needed it to be a success ... And my failure is only proof of the fact that what I was after was unreachable ..."

"I don't understand you . . ."

"So what? To be or not to be a forger, that was the problem, that was the solution, that was the question . . . Maybe it had to kill me, but the only work I could henceforth try to produce had to be my own. I dropped the jigsaw idea, I set out to paint on my own account. I tried, yes, I tried to be the equal of Antonello. Not to employ meticulous and patient care to equal his accuracy and genius, but to set off with no guides apart from his paintings serving as beacons, as distant targets, and to fly towards him, to experience his labour and his triumph. Antonello da Messina and not anybody else. Antonello and not Cranach, Antonello and not Chardin. Because all ambiguity had to be eliminated, because I had to rise to his limitless triumph, his gigantic lucidity, his phenomenal certainty, his in-human strength. His controlling genius. Because what I'd been striving towards for years and years was nothing other than ascension . . . Because that's where the solutions I'd been looking for were to be found . . . Because at the end of the road I'd have found my own face, which is my sincerest ambition . . . Because I needed my own face, my own force, my own light . . . Because the proof and the trial were the only things that would allow me to stop being a forger thereafter. Because if I'd managed it, then by the same token I would have uncovered something beyond specialist knowledge and craft – I'd have found my own sensibility, my own lucidity, my own puzzle and my own solution . . ."

"Why didn't you manage it?"

"Because it was too difficult . . . I wanted my own face and

I wanted the light . . . I wanted my face and I wanted the Condottiere . . . Victory without combat, certainty without mediation,
strength . . . I was cheating again . . . How could I know I would be that
strength? I struggled to prove it . . . But I was frightened. Yes. But
I already knew I was setting out on an impossible adventure . . . I
knew, but I went on nonetheless . . . What did I have to lose? As good
a way as any of coming a cropper? What did I have to lose in the
game? But time went by . . . It really was my own face that I was
putting on the canvas, drop by drop of sweat, but it wasn't the
Condottiere . . . I corrected, began again, paused, backtracked . . . But
it could not be . . . There was not a chance it was going to work . . ."

"Why did you go on?"

"Because I wanted to know . . ."

"Why did you need to come a cropper?"

"No reason . . . Had to get it over . . ."

"Is that why you started drinking?"

"Yes, that's why, and why not? I looked at myself in the mirror
in the middle of the night. That was me. That was my face, and
my year of struggle and sleepless nights, that oak board and that
steel easel, that was my face too, and so were those pots and those
hundreds of brushes and the rags and the spotlights. My story. My
fate. A fine caricature of a fate. That was me: anxious and greedy,
cruel and mean, with the eyes of a rat. Looking like I thought I was a
warlord. Like I thought I was a master of the world at the crossroads
of the universe. Like I thought I was untouchable, free and strong.
That was me. Anxiety, bitterness, panic. You can keep up the illusion

for a minute, but then it all falls down, in one go, everything goes haywire, under the impossible gaze of other people who come roaring over the walls, and they're definitely the winners. So I started to drink, like an animal, like I'd never drunk before, not even two years ago when I was here, because I was in a panic at the mere idea of having to answer Geneviève. I started drinking and pacing up and down in the room. Drinking from the bottle. I broke my brushes, I tore up all the prints I could reach. I drank till I collapsed . . ."

"And Madera didn't say anything?"

"No . . . He called Rufus. Rufus got there that evening. I was asleep. Next morning I left with him for Gstaad, where he was on holiday, for a week's rest."

"Had they seen the Condottiere?"

"Yes."

"Did they say anything?'

"No."

"How so?"

"At first sight it didn't matter if it was a mess or not . . ."

"I don't understand."

"There weren't any mistakes of technique. I had strictly painted an Antonello. All the characteristics were present: only they were crude signs. It worked for a little while; then you could see you'd been duped. It was too facile. Too instantaneous. Hey, look at me, I'm the fearless Condottiere! Ha, I'm a tough guy, have you seen the muscles in my neck? Or else distant in a way that was too artificial. If you just looked at the panel with the idea in your mind that it was not an

Antonello, then the trick was easy to see. The rest of it came by itself. Do you see? That's what a poor forgery is. If I'd done it right, you'd have been able to look at the panel every which way to try to prove it was a fake and not been able to do so. It was logical. It was the most logical thing in the world . . ."

"Do you think you can be a competent judge of that, all by yourself?"

"There's not the slightest doubt. I painted that panel. I believed in it for a long time. I did my utmost with it for as long as I could."

"But during your stay in Gstaad, didn't Madera often look at the painting?"

"No. The panel wasn't quite finished. The background needed another coat and it hadn't yet been varnished so as to produce the craquelure. Before leaving I covered it with a canvas frame because some parts weren't completely dry and I had to prevent dust from getting to them."

"If you'd had to have it authenticated by a specialist, do you think it would have passed?"

"Certainly not. No art critic or expert would have taken more than thirty minutes to see through it . . ."

"What did you plan to do?"

"I don't know . . . I don't remember . . . Lots of things went through my mind. I wanted to have a rest and clear out . . ."

"Did you expect to go back to Dampierre?"

"Yes and no . . . I don't know . . . I wasn't planning on doing anything . . . Oh, I wasn't even thinking about the disastrous thing at all . . . I didn't give a damn . . . I slept, I went skiing, I read detective stories by the fire . . ."

"Why did you go back?"

"It's too complicated to tell you . . . A bad memory . . . I got fed up with skiing . . ."

"Was that a sufficient reason?"

"As good as any other . . . When I left for Gstaad I was almost contented. I wanted to see the snow and go skiing. The snow wasn't very good and there wasn't enough sunshine . . . I was getting bored . . . I went back to Paris."

"Just like that? In the middle of the night on a private plane? Just because the snow wasn't good?"

"Yes . . . All because the snow wasn't good . . . It sounds ridiculous, but that was just about the only reason . . . Gstaad had nothing to do with it . . . It was a different issue. The memory of Altenberg, a small town in Switzerland where I spent a few years at the start of the war . . . That's where I acquired my passion for snow, odd though it may seem . . . I'm putting it badly . . . I mean that, in a certain way and in certain circumstances, I was perfectly happy . . . but in Gstaad I got bored . . . That's all . . ."

"It doesn't make sense."

"Of course it doesn't make sense, but did the desire for the Condottiere make sense? None of it made any sense . . . But all the same that's what I was living in . . ."

"What did you want to do in Paris?"

"Call Madera, to tell him I wasn't coming back to Dampierre, that the Condottiere was hopeless and I didn't give a shit about it, and that he could go jump in a lake ..."

"Did you?"

"No ..."

"Why not?"

"I called Geneviève ..."

"Why Geneviève?'

"The same reason I left Gstaad ... the same reason that spurred me to paint the Condottiere ... No obvious reason ... They were just things I wanted to do ..."

"To provoke a disaster?"

"Probably, but so what? What do you know about it? Why a disaster? It could have worked ..."

"Could Geneviève have responded?"

"Why not? Since I was able to call her. What's so special about picking up the phone? What's so miraculous about answering?"

"Would it have been a miracle if she had answered?"

"Yes ... yes and no ... it wouldn't have made any sense either ... She didn't answer because she understood that I was the person calling her ..."

"Maybe she was out?"

"At three a.m.? No ... She was there ... She'd understood ..."

"How long was it since you'd seen her?"

"A year and a half ... At Rufus's party ..."

"How did you know she'd be at home?"

"It was February, and it was three a.m. . . . . There was no reason for her to have changed her job or her apartment, so she was there ... "

"It doesn't matter anyway ... Why did you call her?"

"To provoke a disaster, like you said ... To have her start hovering over me, being present and imminent and reassuring, with all the spells and tyranny she would bring with her ... "

"Did you want to kill Madera?"

"No ... I didn't want to murder anybody ... "

"What sort of thing was it, the disaster?"

"It wasn't anything ... Things going on like they had, as if nothing had changed, as if nothing had happened ... The eternal return, the same action done over and over again a thousand times, the same pointless patience, the same useless effort ... My own story written down once and for all, in a closed circle, with no way out other than dying ten or twenty or thirty years on. Needing to go on to the end without meaning, without necessity ... "

"Is that what you were thinking?"

"I wasn't thinking anything at all ... I knew, as if I'd always known, as if I'd been trying to forget ... that it wasn't possible ... I'd tried everything. But I'd been caught. Trapped liked a rat. I would go on piling up Grecos and Clouets and Goyas and Baldovinettis until death did us part, without believing in them, without wanting to do it, I would produce a heap of canvases and panels like my own shit, I would go on living off the dead. Until I was dead too ... "

"Why did you kill Madera?"

"I don't know ... If I knew I wouldn't be here ... If I'd known, I suppose I wouldn't have done it . . . You think it's easy . . . You commit an act . . . You don't know . . . you can't know . . . you don't want to know . . . But after a while it's behind you . . . You know you did it . . . and then . . ."

"Then what?"

"Then nothing."

"Why do you say 'you'?"

"No reason . . . It doesn't matter . . . I killed Madera . . . And then? It doesn't make things any simpler . . . A last act, the least act of all . . ."

"Just to see . . ."

"As you say . . . Just to see what would happen . . ."

"And what did happen?"

"You can see that for yourself . . . Nothing yet . . . Perhaps one day something will happen . . . Something worthwhile . . ."

"Are you sorry you killed Madera?"

"No . . . I don't give a damn . . . It's hardly any business of mine . . . I'm not interested . . ."

"What would have happened if you hadn't killed him?"

"I don't know . . ."

"Try to use your imagination."

"I haven't got any imagination . . . Nothing at all would have happened. He would have noticed – if not himself, then Rufus or Nicolas or somebody, or else I'd have told them – that the Condottiere wasn't worth anything . . . They'd have given me something else to do . . . or else they'd have tried to get rid of it as it was . . ."

"As an Antonello?'"

"No . . . They'd have made a convenient discovery of a Master of This or That . . . The Man in Red or something of the sort . . ."

"Would you have carried on after that?"

"I don't know . . . Maybe, maybe not . . ."

"Why did you kill Madera?"

"Because I was sick to the back teeth. Because it was as good a way as any of being shot of it all . . ."

"Being shot of what?"

"Of the crazy life I'd lived for twelve years . . ."

"Did you want to give yourself up to the police?"

"No."

"What did you plan to do, straight afterwards?"

"Hide the body, clean up the blood a bit, and clear off . . ."

"Here?"

"Here or somewhere else . . . It wasn't enormously important . . ."

"How come Otto came back?"

"I've no idea . . . In principle he spends every Monday afternoon in Dreux . . . He must have forgotten something . . ."

"Had you been thinking about killing him for a long time?"

"No . . . Not for long . . . Half an hour, three-quarters of an hour . . . I've no idea . . ."

"Why not?"

"It came to me suddenly, like a cramp . . . Almost like an idea out of the air . . . An image . . . to begin with . . . Something started hovering over me, something possible, something that started speaking all by itself ... It was meaningless, it was babble, but I listened to it nonetheless ... In the state I was in, one action more or less didn't matter a damn ..."

"Were you out of your mind?"

"You could say that ... You could ... Marginally insane ... or rather, it was as if I had lost all will and all memory ... Unwilled, that's what it was. Anything was O.K., anything that came to me was O.K. ... But then that's what I'd been like for years ..."

"What was in your mind?"

"I don't know ... it doesn't matter ... I picked up a razor, folded it in my palm, I started up the stairs, I went into his office ..."

"Didn't you hesitate?"

"No ... It came all by itself ... With no apparent effort ... With no difficulty ... Why not? It was Madera. He was alive. He was going to be dead. I was dead, I was going to be alive ..."

"Why?"

"I don't know, it's obvious ..."

"He had to die for you to live?"

"Yes ..."

"Weren't you alive?"

"Yes, it would seem that I was alive ... You're wearing me out with your stupid questions ... Of course I was alive ... So what? He was alive as well. Now he's dead and I'm still alive. That's it."

"Did he have to die?"

"Yes, sooner or later, like anybody else ..."

"But it was you who had to kill him . . ."

"You worked that out all by yourself, did you? Very clever, you are . . . No, it did not have to be 'you who had to kill him' . . . But since I did it, heigh ho, it's just as well . . ."

"You're not mounting a good defence . . ."

"I don't want to defend myself . . ."

"What were you after? What were you trying to do? What have you got to lose now by giving an explanation? You know full well that you can't turn the clock back. You're standing there stock still, like a statue. You don't even realise . . ."

"What's it got to do with you? You want to understand. I've told you a hundred times already that there was nothing to understand. I was the one who ought to have died. That's what would have been logical. It would have been normal. I should have committed suicide. I had every reason to do so. I was dishonoured. I was a forger who hadn't managed to make a forgery. Fakers breakers. How about that? Couldn't come up with my own Condottiere, so I should have committed hara-kiri. I should have taken my razor between thumb and index finger and run it oh so delicately over my throat. Lost. Done in. Done for. That's what you won't grasp. That everything had hit the rocks, was smashed to smithereens, dead. My hope to live, my hope to be me, my face. Gstaad wasn't what I wanted. Geneviève wouldn't answer. The Condottiere was a mess. Jérôme was dead. I thought I was free but I was being exploited. I thought I was in disguise but my disguise was another face, one that was more true and even more pathetic than the other one. I thought I was in a place of safety but everything was falling on top of me. I had nothing to hang on to. I was alone in the middle of the night in the middle of my prison in front of my own face that I did not want to recognise. You must understand it. Understand that. What was I supposed to do? Run away, right? Run away where? What planet would have me? Tell me that! The only thing I could do was get rid of myself, throw myself out with the rubbish. What difference did it make if I made a bit more wreckage? What difference would it make to me if I blew everything up? He was in his office, the fool, he had no idea. He should have. He should known there was a barrel of high explosive in his basement . . . He did nothing about it. He let me come in. He didn't turn around. He didn't hear me come closer. It was his fault. It was his fault . . . He'd never helped me . . . He'd lumbered me with a Condottiere . . . He'd shut me away . . . He'd taken advantage of me for twelve years, fifteen years . . . He'd turned me into a docile instrument . . . Do you understand him? Do you understand that? As for me I'd been taken in, hook, line and sinker. I didn't exist, I didn't have the right to exist . . . So all of that was rushing around and jostling and exploding somewhere inside my head, like overloud music it was all bursting and disappearing and coming back . . . I was the one who should have died . . . It was me who'd done it all . . . who'd ruined it all . . . But I wasn't alone. He'd looked at me, he'd toyed with me. I didn't give a damn about dying . . . It hadn't occurred to me . . . It didn't matter any more. What I was could never matter anymore. But first, before dying, before dying from it, before it was all over, the ineffable Anatole Madera would be repaid to the last cent for everything he has helped make happen to me. It was cowardly. It was intentional. So what?"

"But you're still alive ..."

Questa arte condusse poi in Italia Antonello da Messina, che molti anni consumò in Fiandra; e nel tornarsi di qua da'monti, fermatosi ad abitare in Venezia, la insegnò quivi ad alcuni sui amici . . .

Antonello da Messina was the son of the painter Salvatore d'Antonio, who was his first teacher. He left for Rome when still very young to complete his education, then went back to Palermo and finally to Naples, where he made the acquaintance of Antonio Solario, known as Lo Zingaro, "The Gypsy", who like him was an apprentice in the studio of Colantonio del Fiore. From then on, Antonello and Lo Zingaro were great admirers of the Flemish and Dutch Schools and tried to imitate their manner, but didn't know what procedures they used and obtained only unsatisfactory results. The sight of a Van Eyck canvas belonging to Prince Alfonso of Aragon made up the young Sicilian's mind. He abandoned all his work in progress and, despite the length and cost of the journey, set off straight away for Flanders to seek out the Master of Bruges, declared his passionate admiration for his work with such convincing enthusiasm that Van Eyck, though initially rather cool, was soon won over by the fiery Mediterranean youth and took Antonello on as a disciple. Antonello's respectful affection and good faith as an artist, allied to his exceptional abilities, soon made him Van Eyck's most favoured pupil, and the master came to have fatherly feelings for the young man who had come from Italy to learn from him the secret of an art that he felt unable to rival. So he revealed the technique of painting in oils, or rather, the practical means of applying it . . .

Questa maniera di colorire accende più i colori, né altro bisogna che diligenza et amore, perché l'olio in sé si reca il colorito più morbido, più dolce, e delicato e di unione e sfumata maniera più facile che li altri . . .

Antonellus Messaneus me pinxit . . . From his eternally frozen haughtiness the Condottiere gazes on the world. His mouth is slightly curved: it's not a smile nor a pout, but perhaps the expression of an unconscious or self-accepting fierceness. Footnote. The Condottiere is not moving: you cannot guess what he might do next, you cannot imagine anything more, or add anything to his sheer presence. Cranach's Philipp Melanchthon is alternately an intelligent gaze, a cunning smile, and firm hands: he is a proper politician. Memling's subject is a praying bull, a mop of hair, a thick neck. Holbein's Robert Cheseman only has the nobleman's superciliousness, the luminous splendour of his costume, and the alertness of a huntsman. The Condottiere is always more than that. He is gazing at all three of them. He could look down on them, secretly or openly. Some day any one of them might have need of him. He does not despise them, that would be beneath him, he is in a stronger position than that: he deals on equal terms with princes, kinglets, bishops and ministers. He goes from town to town with his troopers in tow. He has nothing to lose: no friends, no enemies. He is brute force.

But brute force can be anything. Serenity is not enough.

Certainty is something they all have. Any portrait, any man is always the achievement of some kind of certainty. The Condottiere is beyond that: he has no need to reach towards anything; he's not trying to understand the world, he does not need to understand it. He is not trying to master the world, he already does. He already did. He is The Condottiere. Where is his stance to be found? Nowhere. But it is there, signalled by a look in the eye, by a jaw, by a scar. I am that I am. He is bare. And that is enough. Goya's Don Ramón Satué, in the Rijksmuseum, needs a broad and open shirt collar and a proud yet vaguely approachable posture with his arched back. Chardin needs his spectacles, eye-shade, turban and scarf, with a sharp turn of his head and a cheeky, ironical and penetrating gaze to challenge the fops who stare at his work and provide him with a living. Never will the Condottiere make the slightest movement of that kind. He has understood. He knows. He is in charge. In charge of a world that is collapsing and falling apart, a world of minute size. But that does not matter. He travels the land on horseback. He only stops in princely courts.

Such instant victory is a myth. Yet nobody can resist it. The ineffable Baldassare Castiglione, apparently the greatest Humanist of the Renaissance, has come down to us only in the conventional garb of the wise man: fur bonnet, a fine beard, a brooch and lace doublet. His hands are crossed in a way that suggests understanding. What brings you here, my good man? Cupped hands, one thumb resting on the other. Not yet a Jesuit, but already two-faced; he knows the arts and sciences, mathematics and philosophy. He is on the verge of winking at you. The Condottiere's eyes blaze at him. All he knows of the world is his little scar: see how well I fight . . .

No question that he is what he wants to be – a bad boy. Beside him Botticelli's young man looks almost sickly: a metaphysician tortured by being a virgin. The sole result of immersion in a mystical brine. The Condottiere has no passion, not even for power: that is a game at which he wins every hand. It is not even worth cheating. Not even worth pushing yourself. It is all set up. He is only barely a warlord. Certainly not a madman. Nothing like Saint-Just or Aleksandr Nevsky or Tamerlane. He is neither a Napoleon or a Machiavelli. Nor all in one, because he has no need to define himself. Unity or contradiction. His fate is perfectly laid out. His freedom is entire. He hesitates not at all. His life is an arrow. No ambiguity, no two sides to it. Has he ever had to wonder about anything? No. No trickery. His place was laid down in advance, in a society where the conduct of all men of substance, be they bankers, princes, bishops, patrons, tyrants, or traders, requires the direct intervention of such a man, an independent but obedient instrument who can settle problems for other people, problems that are not and cannot be his own, and who therefore lives his life with a conscience that is entirely adequate to his utter neutrality and completely inaccessible, acknowledging only the law and rights of the one who pays him best . . . Political clashes, economic contradictions, religious tensions and struggles all converge on him, end up with him, and are resolved by him. He is paid to be the scapegoat. He pockets the money. But he has nothing at stake. Why go into battle for business that is not his? Halfway between Venice and Florence, at a meeting that is more comradely than hostile with the chief of another band of marauders who happens to be an old friend, a handshake abolishes the centuries-old stand-off between the Medicis and the grandees of the Signoria. Why should there be a fight? A faked skirmish allowed the two mercenaries to decide, in the light of the politics of the day and their personal interests, which side would be the winner and which would be instantly granted the benefit of a heroic defeat, so as not to damage his career prospects . . .

Was that the source of the irony in his eyes? The Condottiere takes all and gives nothing back. Never committed, never betrayed, never caught off guard. Was that what he had wanted to be? A paradoxical artisan of reconciliation, a geometrical intersection? The man who won every hand?

Why want the Condottiere? Who was the Condottiere? A picture of triumph, or the triumph of painting? Who had set it all out, who had made it perceptible? *Antonellus Messaneus me pinxit.* And there he is, nailed down on the panel, labelled, defined, at last bounded, with his strength, his serenity, his certainty and impassibility. What was art if not that approach, that way of giving a perfect definition of an era, transcending and explaining it at the same time, explaining it by transcending, and transcending it by explaining it? The same movement. Beginning who knows where, perhaps just in the requirement of coherence, and ending up in the total, brutal, decisive mastery of the world . . .

And that was why he was once again a man in pursuit of that

portrait as Chardin and Modigliani had been before him, as had Ingres and David when he'd sketched in an instant as he leaned out of a window the face of Marie-Antoinette on her way to the scaffold, or like any one of those ancient Cambodian sculptors who in his own time and society had also been in pursuit of the essential, to express his own forward path and his ideal as he looked on that amazing chaos – the world – with a perfectly serene, appropriate, lucid, critical gaze . . .

Was that what art was? To summon forth rigour, order and necessity? Exactly how did that come to be his business? How did that justify him? What you did in Split . . .

Gaspard the forger. A trap just too well sprung. It was obvious. The deceptive impression of security. As tempting as a second home. The world kept out. Refusal pure and simple. What had he done in twelve years?

The forger's art is all in pretence. The Hoard of Split was just a few blows of a wooden mallet on sheets of gold and silver, some bronze and copper coins and a coin-punch. Becker had done it better. The slave-smith was a clumsy pretence, a pretence of skill, based on a rough knowledge of the events of the period and approximations of chronology, calendars, gods, and genealogies. The dawn of art . . . What he knew were the assembly instructions. *Gesso duro*. Plaster of Paris, Meudon white, and fish glue. What then? Nothing . . .

*

And then Madera died. Perhaps certainty had no meaning until after an uncertain step? His victory? It was certainly not an instant triumph, in sublime and satisfied serenity – the triumph of a Condottiere – but it was perhaps a new awakening of confidence, wrested from the passage of time in obvious alarm at the possibility of a relapse and in the unknown, misapprehended and finally acknowledged danger of mistakes and missteps, a new assertion of his life, the ultimate wager abolishing chance, tipping the scales, overfilling the cup, in a gigantic collapse of doubts and fears. A first autonomous action, the first act of freedom, the first evidence of a conscious mind . . .

A response? A proof? Not quite, not yet. Maybe. Maybe not maybe. Definitely maybe. Not an elucidation or an explanation or an illumination. His mistake had been to believe that a merely spontaneous and misunderstood act of rebellion could give rise to certainty. That the life he'd denied would magically spring forth from a mere gesture. Years past were dead, and nothing from them would survive henceforth. Because he was not yet dead, what had foundered and gone to the bottom whole and entire was his own past. Perhaps Madera had not had to die, but once he was dead, his own action had to go beyond itself, and become the unavoidable conclusion, the self-evident outcome of a meaningless life. His was the head that had to fall . . .

A wave of panic and sudden mindlessness, by the grace of that other face slowly coming to life on the panel. In the laboratory he had left behind, the failure had been complete. His life, in his own hands. His actions. The ringing of the telephone in the Belgrade studio. All around the globe ... His desperate flight through the streets of Gstaad, running like a shadow, peeling the walls, a black shape in the black night ... Little by little, found guilty with no right of appeal. All hands raised, bar one. His own ...

"I had three rather odd days. I went back to Dampierre and returned to the studio downstairs. I was supposed to finish it all off. I'd asked Madera for a week. We hardly spoke to each other. He left that evening to spend the weekend in Paris. He came back on the Monday at eleven in the morning and I killed him at three. While he was away I'd meant to get back to the painting but I couldn't do it. He'd had every drop of alcohol cleared out of my refrigerator; otherwise I think I would have started drinking again. On Sunday I got hold of a car and went to Paris. Yet again I was on the verge of not going back. I don't know why I did go back. . ."

"What did you do in Paris?"

"I dropped in at my apartment. There was a letter from Rufus saying he would be coming on the Monday. I phoned him in Geneva, where he'd been since a few hours after I left Gstaad, to tell him to come down to Dampierre on Tuesday. I wanted to let him know it was a mess but I didn't dare. I told him it would be finished by the time he got there. He didn't say anything and hung up very quickly . . . I went out and bought some detective novels from one of the booksellers on the *quais*; I went to the Louvre, to the seven-metre gallery, to look at the Condottiere. I stood in front of it for a few seconds, then left. I fetched the car and drove to Versailles and took a walk in the grounds. There was hardly anyone about. I got back in the car and drove to Dreux for dinner. Then back to Dampierre. I read detective stories all night long. I smoked three packs of cigarettes. At six I took a bath. Otto was awake; he asked me if I needed anything from Dreux because he was going over there that afternoon. I told him I didn't need anything. I had some coffee. I took off the canvas frame and looked at the panel for two hours. Then I put the cover back on for the last time. It must have been around ten o'clock. I lay down on the bed, opened another pack of cigarettes and the last of the detective novels I'd bought in Paris. At eleven Madera came back; he called me and asked where I was up to. I told him I would have finished by the evening, that I'd been to Paris the day before, that I'd had a letter from Rufus and that Rufus would be there the next day. He asked me to come up to see him in the afternoon . . ."

"Why?"

"He didn't say . . . It couldn't have been anything very important . . ."

"Did he often summon you by telephone?"

"Now and again . . . He would come downstairs sometimes, in the evening . . . He spent almost every afternoon in his office, presumably to deal with business matters . . ."

"Didn't he have a secretary?"

"He had a secretary in Paris but I never saw him . . . I only found out he had an apartment in Paris late in the day . . . And a dozen others dotted around . . ."

"While you were doing the Condottiere was he regularly in residence at Dampierre?"

"About three-quarters of the time, yes ... He occasionally travelled ..."

"And Otto?"

"Otto stayed at Dampierre all the time. He'd been there five years. He looked after the house when Madera was away ..."

"What about his other houses?"

"I suppose he had other housekeepers ..."

"How long had he been selling fakes?"

"Since 1920. He was barely twenty-five at the time. Rufus had only just been born. Jérôme was only about twenty, too."

"How did it come about?"

"Jérôme was the pupil of Joni Icilio, who was still called Federico. He died in 1946. He was quite clever, but it was an open secret that he did pastiches and he worked mainly as a restorer. I never found out how Jérôme came across him. Apparently around 1920 Jérôme was on the lookout for a fence to handle his work and he stumbled into Madera ..."

"Where did he come from?'

"No idea ... For years I thought he was Portuguese. They started with the Impressionists, Sisleys and Jongkinds that they made and stored in the villa that Madera owned in Tangier, and which then left for Australia and South America in false-bottomed trunks. Over time they perfected their system, taking on intermediaries, salesmen, agents, guys like Speranza and Dawnson, they were so to speak heads of department in charge of a whole network, sometimes a whole country – for instance, Nicolas had Yugoslavia – and they were to be seen in auction rooms, exhibitions, antique dealers, museums, editorial offices, reading all the specialist periodicals. It was fairly simple. When someone was on the look-out for something – a twelfth-century Madonna, a rare stamp, a Cambodian head, a Bantu fetish, a Corot, a Daumier, an anything – then one of the innumerable second or third fiddles dotted around the world would send a note to someone higher up who would pass it on to Madera. The order was placed. A few days or a month, or for larger works a couple of months later, the art lover would be offered a unique opportunity to acquire . . ."

"And the certificate of authenticity?"

"They had them. I never knew where they got them, or whether they were fakes too or whether they had an official authenticator on their books."

"Even for paintings?"

"Even for mine . . ."

"How did Jérôme manage with so many orders?"

"There weren't so many . . . On average, one a month. When there were two, they chose the more interesting one . . ."

"Did it provide a living for the whole organisation?"

"I don't think so. But most of the salesmen did it on the side. I think they got around fifty thousand for each order they placed. There can't have been many guys whose entire income came from Madera."

"And the police never found out anything?"

"Not as far as I know . . ."

"But Madera must have had some way of accounting for his wealth."

"I never knew how he managed that side of things. Rufus didn't tell me . . ."

"When did Rufus come into the picture?"

"In 1940. He was about twenty years old, and had just inherited an art gallery in Geneva, where Jérôme and Madera had taken refuge. At the start I think Madera bought or bailed out the gallery which was on the verge of bankruptcy, and subsequently used it as a front."

"And you became involved in 1943."

"I started my apprenticeship then. I didn't become a forger until 1947 . . ."

"So how many fakes did you do in all?"

"A hundred or more . . . A hundred and twenty, a hundred and thirty . . . I stopped counting early on . . ."

"Did you always like doing it?"

"What an odd question to ask . . . Yes, I always liked doing it . . ."

"Why is it an odd question?"

"It just is . . . Because you know the rest of the story . . . If I'd stopped liking it straight away, then I think I could have stopped doing it . . . But once you get a taste . . . It turned into a kind of habit . . . a way of life, something perfectly natural . . . like breathing or eating. Do you understand?"

"Yes, I understand . . ."

"Even when I knew it was a betrayal, an expropriation, it was nothing to me, it was not my business, because I was no more than a sort of perfect memory, a resurrection . . ."

"Didn't you ever try to paint . . . I mean, to paint for yourself?"

"No . . . never . . . except for the Condottiere . . . right at the end . . ."

"Why don't you say that you knew where you were going when you started the Condottiere?"

"Because it's not as simple as that. I knew and didn't know at the same time. I wanted and didn't want . . . Same old story . . . Safeguards on all sides . . . If I managed it, it would have been what I wanted, I would have cleared the table at a stroke and established the situation; if I failed, it would have been because it was too hard . . . Only it didn't fail in the way I would have preferred . . ."

"Yes . . ."

"Do you see? I did succeed in painting my own portrait . . . I got my own face . . . If I'd tried for the portrait of Dorian Gray I couldn't have done better . . . That's all. He died of it. I did too . . . in a different way."

"The forger in you died . . ."

"The forger is dead, long live Gaspard . . . Sure . . . In a few years, perhaps . . . In a few generations, when all the world's art critics have re-established the truth . . . That's what's hardest, that's what's the most surprising . . . The absence of my life . . . I can't say: the small Madonna of Sienna, that everybody thinks is from the school of Jacopo della Quercia, well, what do you know, it isn't . . ."

"Do you need your past to go on living?"

"The same as everyone else . . ."

"Not everyone demolishes their past the way you did . . ."

"Not everybody has a past like mine . . ."

"That's what I meant . . ."

"Perhaps you're right . . . What do I know, after all? No past and no problems . . . Dead and brought back to life . . . Lazarus Winckler, right? But that's no use, it doesn't lead anywhere either . . ."

"What are you going to do?"

"I don't know . . . I'll never be a forger again, that's all. I'll try not to let myself get caught in a trap of my own making again. I'll try to start from scratch, to find out what got me going, what kept me going . . . I don't know . . . to give my best . . . it doesn't mean much . . . to be clear in my head . . . To try to know myself and to know the world . . ."

"Will you be a painter?"

"I'll try . . . Or maybe not . . . I feel I'm consumed by my own expertise, my patience, my manias . . . My memories and subterfuges . . . I really don't know . . . Why do you want to know?"

"You'll have to start earning a living one day . . ."

"Perhaps . . . It's odd . . . Why am I thinking of a future? Why? It doesn't mean anything . . . It's a word that never did mean anything . . . I was living on the edge of a circle, I went round and round . . . I must have been rotating every three hundred and sixty-five days as well . . . from New Year's Day to New Year's Eve and round we go again . . . From Bosch to Ribera, Fragonard to Chirico . . . Here we go again . . . Doing the same detail a hundred, a thousand times to learn it, then a hundred and a thousand times to get it right . . . It's not hard to become a forger . . . But it's all dead and gone now. Dead like the other guy, the twelve years, the sixteen years, Nicolas, Madera, Otto, Rufus, Dampierre, Split, Geneva, Gstaad. Dead at a stroke. Places of refuge and fear. An unbridgeable gulf. Mila and Geneviève. Forgotten. Murdered. And because of me too, it was the same effort . . . It's funny . . . It was meaningless . . . Twelve years vanishing just like that. One razor slash and splat! Without a word, just like that, at a stroke . . ."

"Did you have to deal the blow?"

"It's possible . . . Hardly . . . I was going up the stairs with my razor in my hand . . . That's all . . . And then I found myself in his study. He was lying on his back. He looked idiotic . . . Completely bewildered, he didn't know what had happened to him . . . I don't know what was going through my mind . . . it wasn't my past nor my future life . . . I think I was badly out of breath . . . I don't know . . . At a stroke . . . oh, for one millionth of a second I was unbelievably happy, incredibly proud . . . He looked so stupid lying there on his beautiful carpet, drowning in his own blood . . . he looked like what he'd always been, a kind of pig, a bloated seal . . . I can't find the right word . . . I don't want to be stupid or mean . . . I don't want to fabricate . . . I don't want to be in bad taste . . . At a stroke . . . as if the roles had been reversed, as if I'd done something natural . . . as if I'd done something natural for the first time in my life . . . Do you see? As if everything was changing, as if it was all falling to pieces and nothing would be the same again, I didn't recognise myself any longer, I didn't understand myself anymore ... I don't want to offer another lame excuse ... I don't want to cheat again ... You know what I mean ... It was as if the Condottiere himself was dead as well, along with my obsessions and my fear. It was as if with the collapse of the last bastion of my defences the reasons why I had constructed them were also falling to the ground ... Perhaps that's what I failed to understand ... Perhaps that's why in a flash I felt so happy ... It was like the world was falling down, but not falling on top of me, not burying me in its ruins, but instead opening up a vista that had been blocked for ages, as if I'd suddenly come to the top of a mountain before dawn and all at once was able to see the sun rising ..."

"That was Altenberg, wasn't it?"

"It was ... But my mistake was to believe that things could wait. And be resuscitated at will. To believe that the world had been frozen into place the day I became a forger. That was absurd. Gstaad wasn't Altenberg. Geneviève wasn't answering. And the long-cherished illusion of my victory had hit the rocks with the Condottiere ... The world was on the move. I thought I was safe but my shell was stifling me, my ivory tower was cutting me off. I didn't realise. It was a weird existence. So false. So much more false than what I wanted. False inside its own falseness, do you see? A life with no roots and no connections. With no past beyond the abstract, mummified past of the world, like a museum catalogue. A paltry universe. A camp. A ghetto. A prison. The fragile interest of fakery, luxury ... But it cost me too dear ... It wasn't a profession, it wasn't a way to pay the rent, it wasn't a trade ... despite myself, it had become my whole life. My *raison d'être*. My calling card. Gaspard Winckler, Forger. My definition. Absurd, unproductive, inefficient. A life that day after day was suffocating me because I needed something else, and the increasingly powerful feeling that nobody could or would come to my aid . . . The ever more stressful conviction that the malady was inside me, a malady of dissatisfaction and boredom, to which Rufus, Jérôme, Madera and everyone else had sentenced me . . . They didn't lift a finger. They strapped me down. I couldn't refuse, I couldn't say no, I couldn't tell them I was going to drop it. It was total and utter dependency. An entirely inextricable relationship. A Gordian knot. It couldn't be undone by actions or by words. It couldn't be remedied by dabs of pigment, by oils, by canvases. There was nothing to be done, do you see? I had to stay or run away. But I couldn't run away. It had been too long. It was too late. I was too scared. I was too young. I was too old. Any old excuse . . . I said yes. My life became unbearable and I didn't know it, I didn't want to know, things fell over, went rotten, sank. I was still there, unmoved, blind . . . It all had to go up with a bang, at a stroke. To burst. Yes, at last, hands had to be raised, I had to wake from my sluggishness, from my game-playing, from my sleep. I had to strip off my masks and rise up against that man like a hairy, violent, unrestrained and fearsome monster. Revolt. Revolution. Freedom fight. Whatever. The battle . . . He died. And that's enough. He is dead and all is well. Even if I'd lost, even if Otto had got me, even if I'd been turned over to the police, even if I'd been sentenced, it wouldn't matter. I had to kill him. His blood had to flow and flood the room, I had to be happy that he'd died, I had to live because of his death. I killed Madera and I'm proud of it, I assert it, and I shout it from the rooftops, and I'll yell it out. I needed to kill him. For years it had been necessary for him to die, it had to be possible all the same for me to refuse the yoke, the servitude, despite everything, in spite of myself, thanks to me, beyond me. I had to shake my head. I had to say no. I should have picked up the blasted telephone and shouted all my anger at him, my despair, my weariness, my conviction. I killed him without saying a word, like a coward. I didn't dare burst out laughing. Never mind. I understood and that's what matters. Yes, I was the victim and he was the oppressor, I was the slave and he was the master, I was the serf and he was the squire. I owed him everything. He'd taken me on, he'd given me a living. I lived only through him, but I had the strength to get up and kill him, the strength to get rid of him . . . to rise up against him, against everything he provided, help, forgiveness, lucre, food, understanding . . . He hovered over me like a vulture, but I wrung his neck and knocked him off his perch . . . He provided me with a living but I didn't exist. I was my own prisoner, but he was too much of a jailer. He died and I won . . . For sixteen long years my life was like a dream. A bad dream. A bizarre nightmare. Throughout the whole story I was looking for my own face and I found it. He ought to have understood that his last hour was upon him. He should never have called me . . . I went upstairs, with the razor in my hand, panting, impatient, boiling over, I went through the door that was already ajar, I padded across the carpet in his study, I was behind him, staring at the back of his fat red neck, I grabbed him by the forehead and yanked his head backwards. The most wonderful thing in the world. My right hand came down nearer to him and I slashed him at a single stroke . . . All the violence and all the energy of all those years came together . . . I was brave enough, yes, brave enough to be done with it! *Je ne regrette rien!*"

The Condottiere never moves, will never move. He is ineradicable and in his palpable perfection he strikes terror as he gazes upon the world with the cold eyes of a judge. You got fascinated by those eyes, when you should have tamed them, explained them, overcome them and pinned them down on your panel. *Antonellus Messaneus me pinxit.* The Condottiere is not human. He knows neither struggle nor action. Behind his pane of glass, on the other side of the red velvet line, he has ceased to be alive once and for all time. He is not breathing. He does not feel pain. He knows nothing. You tried to reach out to him and to begin with you believed it was reaching him that mattered. But the only thing that mattered was your reaching towards him, the simple gesture, the forward thrust of your body, of your mind, your will and your effort. What you will reach one day after years and years of experiment and invention will lie somewhere else, after blind fumbling, exhaustion, and starting over for the twentieth or one hundredth time in search of your own truth, in pursuit of your own experience, in search of your own life. The world at your feet. Ghirlandaio, Memling, Cranach, Chardin, Poussin. The world at their feet. You will only get there at the end of a strenuous march, like the team that at the start of July 1939 did indeed reach a long-sought vista near the summit of the Jungfrau and suddenly, forgetting its fatigue, was filled to the brim by the blazing joy of sunrise and the radiant revelation of the other side of the mountain, the watershed . . .

The Condottiere does not exist. Only someone called Antonello da Messina. And like him you will seek out the order and coherence of the world that there is. Seeking truth and freedom. In that accessible hereafter lie your time and your hope, your conviction and your experience, your lucidity and your triumph.

Perhaps it is a matter of uncovering the obvious necessity of men in their faces. Perhaps it is a matter of uncovering the obvious necessity of the world in material objects and landscapes. Perhaps it is a matter of uncovering in things and beings, in eyes and gestures, the obvious necessity of triumph. Perhaps. Perhaps not perhaps. Perhaps definitely. Definitely definitely. Dive into the centre of the world. Definitely. To the roots of the unexplained. To the explicable roots. Definitely. Into the unfinishedness of the world. Definitely. Into the world that remains to be possessed and to be built. Definitely. Dive. Push on. Definitely. Towards that perpetual *reconquista* of time and life. Towards that palpable lucidity. Towards that sensibility in full bloom. Dive. Definitely. Dive. Towards the light waiting to be born.

Paris
Navarrenx
Druyes-les-Belles-Fontaines
1957–1960

GEORGES PEREC, born 1936, decided to be a writer at around the age of eighteen, but had a day job as a librarian in a medical research laboratory for most of his adult life. He made his first impact in 1965 with a barely fictional portrait of his own generation, *Things*. Shortly after, he joined Oulipo, the experimental "workshop" for mathematics and literature founded by Raymond Queneau and François Le Lionnais, of which he became the most ardent and celebrated doyen. He is the author of *A Void*, a novel written without the letter "e", of the semi-autobiographical *W or The Memory of Childhood*, and, most famously, of *Life A User's Manual*, hailed by Italo Calvino as "the last real 'event' in the history of the novel so far". He lived in Paris, and died of lung cancer in 1982. *Portrait of a Man*, written in 1960, remained unpublished in French until 2012. This is its first English publication.

DAVID BELLOS teaches French and Comparative Literature at Princeton University. He is the author of *Georges Perec: A Life in Words* and of *Is That a Fish in Your Ear? The Amazing Adventure of Translation*. He has also translated many novels from French, including works by Fred Vargas, Ismail Kadare, Daniel Anselme, Georges Simenon and most especially Georges Perec. He is currently working on a study of Victor Hugo's *Les Misérables*.